ANCIENT REUNION

Book Two:
Lusio

SUE PATERSON

Copyright © 2022 by Sue Paterson All rights reserved.

No part of this book may be reproduced in any form or by any electronic or mechanical means, including information storage and retrieval systems, without written permission from the author, except for the use of brief quotations in a book review.

Cover Design: Matt Hall at Java Press

Interior formatting by Rachel Bostwick

DEDICATION
To Charley and Phillip

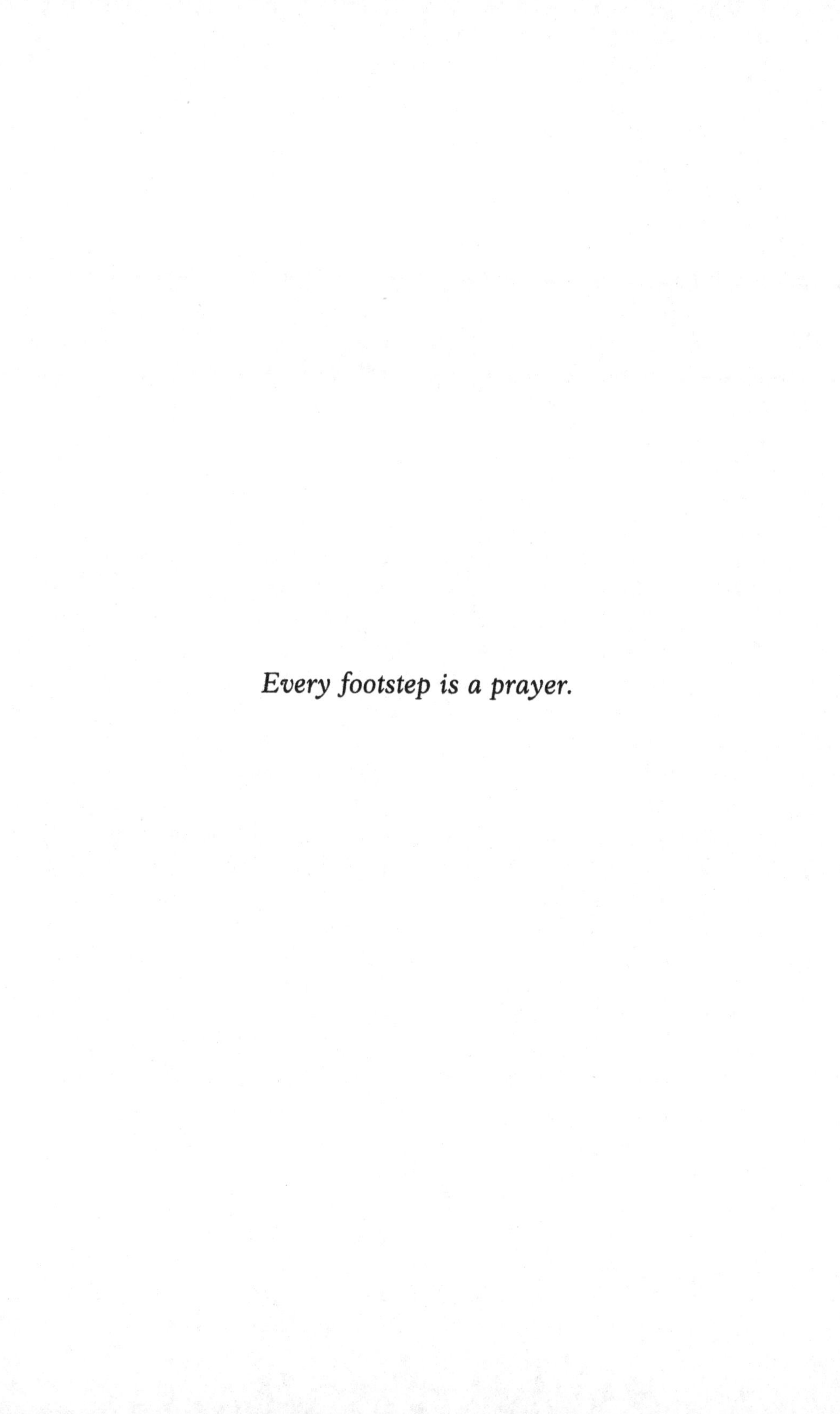

Every footstep is a prayer.

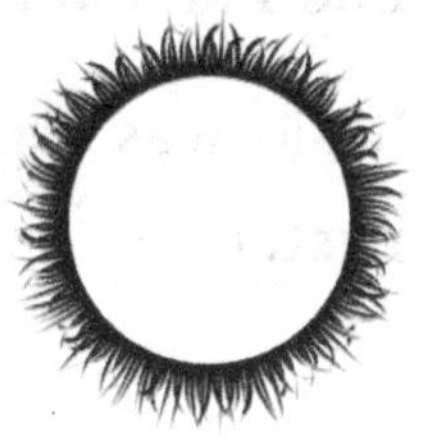

ONE

The afternoon sun hot on his back, dust swirled around Lusio's feet as he neared the bottom of the mountain trail. Shoulders slumped, left foot dragging, his mouth watered in anticipation of soup in his belly as he approached the narrow path leading into the village.

Will they welcome me back?

Memories of their camaraderie and laughter had gotten him through the hardship of the last few months. Since leaving, Lusio questioned if he would ever see his village again. He missed the warmth of his wife with their furs wrapped around them as they slept. The night before he left, they stood hand in hand by the river, watching the sunset, the damp grass tickling their bare feet.

Aiyani.

Six moons ago, two men, strangers to the tribe, came through, asking him to guide them through the mountains. The way they looked at the women in the tribe made his skin crawl, and though they called themselves traders, no interest was shown in the skins and herbs sought after by most. Rumors of deserters from the Spanish Army made him hesitant to leave. Still, Lusio was eager for these men to be gone, and they were persistent.

"Come on, now." Tix, the taller of the two men, let his backpack fall open, exposing a cache of colored beads and trinkets. "Get us over those mountains lickety-split. You'll be back before anyone knows you're gone. Right, Shorty?" Tix grinned at his partner, wiping the spittle darkened by tobacco running out the side of his mouth with his shirt sleeve.

"Snow soon, not safe." Lusio turned to walk away, but the men wouldn't give up.

"Ya knows those renegade soldiers rumored about? What they do to your womenfolk and their young 'uns?" Shorty kicked a stone with his boot, then leaned down and met Lusio's stony gaze. "Ain't a pretty sight."

Tix leaned in close and whispered: "We could take 'em out before they come here."

Raven walked by, a wary look on her face. Lusio noted how their eyes followed his daughter, the hair on the back of his neck bristling at the thought of someone hurting his family. He looked at the mountains, then at the chattering women and children, knowing they wouldn't be able to defend against such an attack. Lusio looked away, but not before the men saw wavering in his eyes and followed him. "Come on man, gotta get over the mountains before it snows."

Rumors of soldiers deserting the Spanish Army were new. The tribe always found fertile land near a river, peacefully settling for extended periods, protecting their own from aggressive tribes. But the brutality of the soldiers scared him. In the end, he agreed to go, hoping to be home by the time the moon became full again.

Days later, as they began their descent to the other side of the mountain, Lusio sensed something was wrong. Except for a large black crow, who screeched a warning from the treetops, nature was quiet. Too quiet. Small animals who would usually skitter out of the way at their approach lay hidden in the grass. Lusio lagged, watching the two continue. Hat slung on his back, Tix stopped now and again to spit tobacco juice on the ground. Shorty plodded along next to him, smoothing his hands through greasy, brown-slicked hair. The men carried on about the corn beer they drank in a previous village, hoping for more in the next. Laughter dying on his lips, Shorty stopped and turned, looking at Lusio. "Come on, now. Stop yer dawdling."

"What's up, Shorty?" The tall man looked back at Lusio, steely blue eyes full of contempt.

"Danger." Lusio gestured around him. "Not safe, turn back."

The men laughed at his words. "Afeard of a bear?" Tix smirked, exposing stained, dirty brown teeth.

"Yellow-bellied fool," Shorty mumbled under his breath. "Come on now," he yelled, hand on the knife strapped to his belt. "Stop yer dallying. Let's go."

Lusio picked up his step. The men continued their banter as the rough trail zig-zagged towards the bottom of the mountain, occasionally looking over their shoulder with a scowl.

Moments later, Lusio froze at a sudden stillness in the air. He stepped behind a mesquite bush and stared at the backs of the men as they approached the widening of the trail. Suddenly, rogue soldiers, hidden by an outcropping of rocks, rushed out. Lusio crouched down and watched Shorty's pants darken with urine as a soldier grabbed him from behind, slitting his throat. Tix dove into the brush, trying to escape, but the deserters were faster, catching his foot. His boot came off, and he clawed at the bush, desperate for a way out. Grabbing his shirt, the soldier yanked him out and threw him into the arms of the other soldier. Blood poured out, soaking the shirts of the two men and the ground they fell on.

Wild-eyed, the renegades ransacked their packs, beads, and trinkets falling to the ground. "Victoria!" One of them bellowed, holding Shorty's knife to the sky. Lusio didn't hear the third man sneak up behind him.

"Look what I found," the third soldier yelled, giving a tug to Lusio's long hair. "Mucho dinero hay esto." The other soldiers laughed, wiping the blood on their pants.

Captured, the soldiers put a rope around his waist, dragging him along the trail. By day's end, they had already begun the ascent of the next mountain, and one day blurred with the next until Lusio lost count of time. They traveled south, following the river until it came to another pass through the next mountain. The soldiers tossed a coin each night to decide who would remain awake, guarding Lusio.

"Mierdo," the unlucky soldier growled. He spat on Lusio before tying his leg to a large rock. Forced to remain awake, the soldier waited for any excuse to kick or beat him more.

When Lusio slept, he dreamt of his wife, Aiyani, standing on the path leading out of the village, watching for his return. In another dream, he heard the laughter of his son Chitto and how it filled the air with joy. And in yet another, he saw his oldest daughter, Raven, walk past the men. Awake, he replayed the day he left the village over and over in his head. The belt around Raven's slender waist was tight, her belly round.

With child? He and Aiyani had given their blessing and knew she would marry Strong Eagle. *Have I missed it?*

His mind wandered to his younger daughters. Around the fire, heads close together, he and Aiyani watched Morning Dove make eyes at Running Elk, giggling at the reminder of their courtship days. And little Aponi. Her smile would brighten the darkest day. She was like a butterfly, magical and bright. Thinking of his family, he would smile at the sunrise, but then the familiar snort and the extra hard jerk on the rope that tied his ankle to the rock would come.

On nights that he lay awake, Lusio kept his eyes closed, waiting for the guard to fall asleep and a chance to escape. One such night, he heard the soldier get up and felt a hard kick on his leg. Lusio rolled his head to the side, feigning sleep. The soldier kicked him harder. Moaning, he curled away but then, through squinted eyes, watched the soldier walk away and soon heard the splash of urine against a tree. Sitting up in the dark, at the crunch of returning footsteps, he slipped the rope off his ankle and slid down into the ravine, hidden in the brush.

The soldiers argued and fought as they scrambled to find Lusio. "Idiota!" One yelled, punching the soldier charged with guarding their captive in the face.

Losing his balance, the soldier slipped into the ravine, feet dangling inches from Lusio's head. "Por favor," the dangling man begged. The soldier that threw the punch glared down and spat, kicking at his comrade's hand, grasping the root of a mesquite bush, hands bleeding from the thorns. "No... por favor." Desperate to find a foothold, the soldier kicked. Inches away, Lusio crouched under the brush, holding his breath as loose stones rolled down the ravine.

The soldier above stood silent, listening. "Todo bien." He relented, pulling his comrade up.

Lusio remained huddled under the mesquite brush while the men looked for him. After a day of searching, they gave up.

"Vamos, se ha ido." Lusio listened to the crunch of the soldier's boots walking away. He waited until nightfall to pull himself up and over the edge. The pain in his ankle almost unbearable, he forced himself to climb the mountain where he found a stream hidden in the trees to settle for the night. Reluctant to have a fire, he caught a fish and ate it raw, spitting out the rough, scaly skin caught in his teeth. Raking pine needles and leaves into a pile, he buried himself, then attempted to sleep, shivering in the cold mountain air.

When the sun rose the following day, he was surprised to see the mesas of his youth in the distance. They'd traveled far. Desperate to return to the northern tribe he called family for the last sixteen years, he knew his legs would not carry him that far. His childhood village was close. It had been years since he'd been banished, so perhaps he would be allowed to return. With doubt dogging every step, Lusio continued. And now, four moons later, it was the last leg of a long journey home.

This morning he awakened to the hoot of an owl. Northern relatives would say it was a harbinger of death, but relatives to the south would disagree, saying owl medicine would bring great vision. He didn't know what to believe anymore. Midday, the sun beating down, Lusio stood on the path, body bent with fatigue. Wiping the burning sweat out of his eyes with his bandana, he jumped back in surprise as a coyote darted out of the grass, crossing his path from east to west. It stopped and stared him in the eye before disappearing. Lusio's eyes searched the brush, trying to see where it went, but only saw golden shimmers of sunlight radiating like spikes out of the dried summer grass.

Am I seeing things? What message did coyote bring? A warning?

A sense of foreboding ran through him and he closed his eyes, his mind flooded with the shrill voice of storytellers from his childhood. "Stop and pray to the spirits of the west.

Ask them to take pity on you. An offering of corn pollen to coyote might leave you in peace." Mouth dry, Lusio reached for his waterskin. Empty. Ignoring the coyote's warning and the storyteller's teachings, he took a step forward.

What else can happen to me?

Driven by hunger and fatigue, determined to make it to the village before sunset, he ignored the ominous feeling lurking in the back of his mind. Bad luck might find him up the trail, but today he would chance it. Lone Elk would pray for him and appease the spirits. But throughout the day, he couldn't shake the feeling. Passing under a grove of cottonwoods, yellowed leaves fell and brushed his shoulders before fluttering randomly to the ground. He stopped and looked towards the mountains in the south.

What was different? Something... He felt it in his bones like one feels the rain coming.

Stepping onto the narrower dirt path, a shiver ran through him as he touched the cool red, jagged rock cliffs to his right. The ravine dropped off sharply on his left, scattered with mesquite and juniper brush covering the cracked earth. He was close. His heart pounded. Stopping, he raised his hands to cup his mouth and made the call of a dove. His feet sweat in his moccasins as he waited.

Wonder how much Chitto has grown after all these moons? He looked forward to sweeping his son into his arms, their laughter filling the air. *Will he think he's too big for such a thing?*

The laughter. He missed that the most. It could fill one with joy, even on the hardest of days. He cupped his hands and called again, flickering his fingers to draw out the sound. Looking up at the clifftop, he expected to see Running Elk's face pop over, greeting him with his crooked smile. But no one appeared. Belly taut with fear, he continued. Around the last bend, a breeze dried the sweat on his forehead. His stomach clenched at the pungent, sweet scent of death, threatening to spew out the little he'd eaten. Sounds of flies drew his attention to the steep ravine. Bodies of dead soldiers lay, eye sockets empty, dismembered, and chewed on by animals. Recognizing the few bits of clothing remaining on the soldiers, he spat on the ground, anger running through him like a hot fire.

TWO

It was the same monsters. They came back here after I escaped...

Scattered footprints of moccasins and boots showed signs of fighting. Lusio's heart reached out with lingering hope, but as the hair prickled on the back of his neck, the icy feeling in the pit of his stomach told him he was wrong. Silently, Lusio retraced his steps. A little way back, he found a crevice and using outcrops of rocks, climbed to the top. Grimacing in pain, he crawled to the edge on the other side and peered over. Seeing no movement, body heavy with dread, he eased his way down and into the coolness of the trees. Broken branches and more signs of struggle lay in the woods behind the community fire pit. On the ground was an impression the size of a child, surrounded by handprints.

Stepping into the camp, he saw the familiar log where Lone Elk, chief of the tribe, sat to greet newcomers. The spot, worn bare by years of sitting, was empty. Fresh ash remained in the community fire pit, but the cooking pots were gone. Nearby, a mound topped with stones in the shape of a Sacred Circle stood. At each corner, small, blackened piles of ash remained where fires once burned. His heart stopped as he realized bodies lay under the stones. *Spirits have left their bodies and flown away. But how? And why?*

To his left, a dried corncob was tied to the front of a tree with a strand of leather. A memory was etched in his brain of Chitto and his friends throwing pretend arrows, longing for the day they would be old enough for their own bows. Lusio shook his head to clear the images and deny the reality of what was in front of him. A breeze tousled his hair, which lay loose around his shoulders. Sensing a presence behind him, he swirled around, his heart skipping a beat.

"Aiyani?" He could feel her on his skin as a whiff of lavender brushed by him. She always had the uncanny knack of approaching from behind, steps so gentle he didn't know she was there. But at the sight of empty space, Lusio fell to his knees, retching. *This can't be happening. Please, Spirit, let this be a dream.*

But as the sun drifted west, the air cool on his skin, he knew it wasn't. Laying on the ground, shadows of dusk approaching, he felt someone lay a hand on his shoulder, then a feather-like brush on his cheek. Startled, Lusio rolled onto his back, squinting into the fading light. Above him, the oak tree shed leaves in the evening breeze, brushing his face like whispers as they fell on and around him. The small branch above him, almost bare, wobbled. A yellow-bellied chickadee sat watching him. He stared in surprise as the

bird flew away. Legs shaky, he stood and walked through the village in stunned silence. Someone survived to bury the dead.

Who? How many?

THREE

Dust swirled under the mule's hooves, ribbed and hardened from traversing the mountains. Comforted yet fatigued from the weight of the load on his long back, his black, velvety nose twitched as the dust tickled. His lips trembled in anticipation of the soft, wet grass along the trail. Snorting and shaking his head, Willie wandered over and began to nibble.

Andre turned at the pull on the lead and held his hand up. "Willie needs a rest." He smiled at Aponi, curled up in a fur on the back of the mule. Sleepy-eyed, with the innocence and joy of a child, she sat up and leaned over, wrapping her arms around Willie's neck, nuzzling her nose into his thick, short mane. The mule brayed softly at her touch and buried his snout back into the tall grass.

Andre watched as Jacqo playfully tugged on Morning Dove's braid, his hands brushing her cheek. He was losing him. Jacqo, eyes filled with laughter, looked up and met his brother's gaze, the laughter in his eyes dimming. Andre knew Jacqo wanted to be with Morning Dove, and his hopes of finding their people out east and settling down sunk a little more each day.

Willie perked up his ears, staring down the trail. "What is it?" Andre asked. The mule lifted his head, eyes alert, ears perked. Andre tossed the lead to Jacqo, pulled the musket out of the leather holster, and took off jogging down the trail.

Around the bend, Andre froze. A puma lay on the ground, a spear sticking out of its side. Nearby stood Strong Eagle and Raven, stunned as a young wolf crept between them, growling, teeth bared. Andre pulled the musket up, nestled it into his shoulder, and aimed it at the wolf.

"No," Raven screamed, jumping between them.

In a blur of motion, Strong Eagle rushed him, pushing the musket up. Andre's ears rang, and the smell of gunpowder filled the air. He stood dumbfounded. The wolf ran into the brush, and Strong Eagle went to Raven, pulling her into his arms. Heart pounding, Andre's breath came in gasps as he bent over, hands on his legs.

Morning Dove and Aponi came running around the bend and skidded to a stop, wide-eyed at the sight of Raven in Strong Eagle's arms. And then, shrieks and laughter as

Raven brushed past Andre and collapsed in a pile with her sisters.

Suddenly, pounding hooves came down the trail. Willie raced by in a cloud of dust, the travois teetering, then falling to the side, the contents scattering. "God darn it, ya crazy mule, stop!" Jacqo yelled, close behind. But the mule was determined and kept running, his lead flying behind him, the brothers in hot pursuit.

Moments later, they returned. "Damn mule." Andre tied Willie's rope to a branch nearby. The brothers turned and stood, taking in what seemed more like a dream. Hat in hand, beads of sweat covering his bald head, Andre spun long, red strands of his beard around his finger, transfixed by the sight of the sisters. *So like their mother... I wish you could see this, Aiyani...*

"Better do something with the puma." Jacqo's voice snapped Andre out of the trance, and he shook his head, chasing out the thoughts.

"Right." Andre pulled the spear out of the big cat and tossed it on the ground. The brothers pulled the animal over to a circle of grass and began skinning it.

FOUR

Strong Eagle picked up the spear covered with puma blood, the sticky liquid staining his fingers as he traced them along the edge. Past days and weeks blurred as he looked over at the sisters, tangled in a web of arms wrapped around each other, excited shrieks of joy filling the air.

Raven, she's real. I found her.

Over in the grass, Andre and Jacqo, working in perfect sync, skinned the puma's body. Nearby, Willie the mule, flecks of foam stuck on his snout, looked around and then snorted, sticking his nose back into the grass.

We're all that's left. Had they not come along when they did.... Bending over, Strong Eagle gathered the broken bow and arrows, but when he stood, his head spun and images blurred. *Evil spirits, why are you stalking me... why do you want to control my mind and heart?*

Something cold and wet pressed against his leg, penetrating the icy numbness he felt inside. Strong Eagle stared down into the piercing eyes of Little Wolf, whose eyes changed from a pup into the eyes of Lone Elk. "I'm sorry, father," Strong Eagle whispered, falling into a heap on the ground.

"Strong Eagle!" Andre ran to his friend, his hat dropping on the ground. Raven looked over and jumped up, running to her lover's side. "Needs food and water." Andre glanced over at Jacqo, who pulled a waterskin off the travois, tossing it to his brother.

Morning Dove squatted next to Raven. "He's eaten little since the massacre, said he wouldn't stop until he found you." The wolf pup nosed his way in.

"Little Wolf, no." Raven pushed him away. Pulling jerky out of her pocket, she tossed it to Morning Dove. "Give him this." Aponi joined them and put her arms around the pup's neck, whispering in his ear.

Wide-eyed, Morning Dove held a piece out, smiling at the tickle as he nuzzled it out of her hand.

"Strong Eagle." Raven shook him again, her knees pressed into the dirt as she leaned down and lay her head on his chest. "Wake up."

Strong Eagle pushed her away and sat up. "Raven?" Squinting against the bright sunlight, he looked around at the group, dazed.

"You blacked out," Andre said. "Need to drink." He squatted and held his head steady as Raven drizzled water into his mouth. Strong Eagle drank, then wrapped his arms around his knees, laying his head on them.

"More." Raven lifted his head and pressed the waterskin to his lips. "I thought I lost you forever." Strong Eagle held her gaze for a moment, then dropped his head back to his knees. Raven cupped his chin, pulling his face up. "Every day, I stood by the trail, watching and hoping. But no one came." Voice cracking, she pleaded. "Now you're here. Please, Strong Eagle."

"I should have been there for you." He reached out, caressing her cheek. "I'm sorry."

"Can you stand?" Jacqo held out his hand to help him up. Strong Eagle nodded, but his legs buckled.

Andre took Strong Eagle's arm. "Raven, where to?" Parting the brush, she led them into the clearing.

"I got this," Jacqo called out. Picking up the spear, he tucked it into a pack on the mule. "Ready, Willie?"

Aponi giggled at Willie's snort as Morning Dove stood on her tiptoes, holding the long branches high. Jacqo led the mule through the narrow opening, but the prickly brush snagged the travois. Squeezing underneath, Morning Dove freed it, her face growing hot as she looked up and met

Jacqo's smile. Aponi whispered into Etu's ear and giggled as Little Wolf followed, nuzzling her hand for more jerky.

"Over here," Raven yelled. They joined the rest of the group, who sat in a grassy area in the shade. Raven knelt in front of Strong Eagle, taking his hands. "I'm going to get some food." She leaned in and kissed him, then looked up. "Morning Dove, help me."

Scrambling up the rocks after Raven, Morning Dove looked around, inspecting the food cache and stacks of rabbit skins. "You did all of this?"

"Yes." Raven pulled meat and fish out of the food cache. "I didn't think anyone would come. I had to survive." She pulled out dried chokecherries from a basket. "Ready?"

The girls climbed down the rocks, taking care not to drop anything, and put out the food for the group. Little Wolf sat nearby with a hopeful look in his eyes. Raven laughed and tossed him a bit of jerky. Strong Eagle sat stony-faced, chewing. "Thank you, Raven. Where did you get this?"

"I've been hunting and fishing, like you taught me." Raven looked up at him. "When no one came, I prepared to leave, to go south and find my father's people. Little Wolf and I were going to leave in the morning."

Strong Eagle looked over at the wolf pup, then up at Raven. Without a word, he tipped the waterskin, drained it, and stood. Still unsteady, Andre held out his hand.

"It's okay." Strong Eagle held his hands up in protest. Silently, he walked over to the travois Raven built, looking up as she came and stood by him. He pulled her close, burying his face in her hair, and whispered: "What made you come down the trail today?"

"There was a noise in the bushes, and the branches moved even though there was no breeze." She hesitated. "I found tracks of a large animal earlier, and Little Wolf was restless. Usually, in the mornings he wanders off, but today he stayed close."

"The Puma, it was tracking us." Strong Eagle looked at her. "It led me to you." Then he pulled away and lowered his eyes.

"What is it?" she tilted his face with her fingers. "What's wrong?"

"I was afraid you were hurt or injured... hungry and cold." He pulled her into a hug. "I will never let you go again."

Andre and Jacqo emptied the travois and stood the poles up for the teepee in the grassy area. "The girls can sleep here," Andre yelled, unfolding the leather hide. "But ya'll better do something with the meat."

Morning Dove gathered the organs from the puma. "Aponi, help me with these."

Strong Eagle stroked Raven's face, kissing her forehead. "I'll help Andre and Jacqo." She stared at his slumped shoulders as he walked away. *Something is wrong.*

Raven stared a moment longer, then turned and took the meat up to the smoking pit. Removing the dried fish and rabbit, she wedged more wood under the stones and watched it blaze up, her hand drifting to the talisman in her pocket. Pulling out the small gray stone, she let the sadness and worry which filled her flow into the stone. *Mama, what can I do?*

The stone caught a flicker of sunlight, and feeling reassured, she put the talisman back into her pocket and turned to the fire. Juices from the meat sputtered as she lay strips across the hot stones, covering them with pine boughs. As smoke trickled through the branches, Raven stood on the ledge and looked down as her sisters came through the trees, Little Wolf close behind. They laid the clean organs, translucent in the sunlight, on the ground near the travois to dry.

Morning Dove looked up at Raven and smiled. Climbing the rocks, she joined her as Raven lay more pine boughs over the smoking meat. "I still can't believe you did all this by yourself."

"Come." Raven pulled Morning Dove by the hand. Together they sat on the rock ledge. Feet dangling, they laughed as Aponi hid behind the trees, trying to fool Little Wolf. But he always found her, causing a ripple of laughter to fill the air as she ran and hid again. Strong Eagle stopped what he was doing and looked around the clearing until his eyes found them. Raven started to smile but stopped when she saw a hardened look flash in his eyes. She looked over at Morning Dove, then looked away.

"What?"

"I don't know. The sound of your voice, Aponi's smile..." Raven shook her head. "I never thought I would see you or hear your voice again. I am full of joy, yet it feels strange." Hesitating for a moment, she turned to her sister. "He's different."

Morning Dove paused, watching the scene below. "It's been hard for all of us. But Strong Eagle? He's been quiet, was always gone, and never slept in camp. He went to the rocks at night."

"If I stayed hidden for a day... I could... have... helped." Raven looked away, voice cracking, her face red with shame.

"What happened to you?"

"Strong Eagle woke me and told me to go to the rocks and wait for him." Raven's voice was so quiet Morning Dove had to lean in to hear. "I heard the clash of weapons... everyone was screaming. Mama came running through the trees... I saw her fall and ran to her." Raven shivered. "A man staggered towards us. He was covered in blood and held a hatchet over his head. The look in his eyes... I was so afraid." Morning Dove nestled closer.

"I hid behind a tree, and when he turned and walked away, I ran to the rocks. The next morning I came back. Chitto's body lay by the tree. I looked over and saw your arm under Lomasi's body." Raven squeezed her sister's hand. "The bracelet I made was on your wrist... I thought you were dead." She glanced away. "Everything seemed to be happening so slowly. I stepped towards you, but then I heard men's voices in the woods, getting closer. I was scared and ran. I'm sorry."

Morning Dove leaned into Raven's shoulder. "Strong Eagle said Jacqo found me lying underneath Lomasi... my best friend." Her voice broke. "I'll never see her again."

Raven put her arm around her sister.

"The last thing I remember was putting the kettle on the fire to make tea," Morning Dove said. "Strange men with knives and hatchets came shrieking out of the darkness." Her voice caught. "Mama called out to me. I looked up as she ran towards the teepees and tried to follow but tripped and fell. That's all I remember. Lomasi must have fallen on top of me. She saved me."

"I am grateful to Lomasi." Raven pulled back and looked at her sister. "Are you okay?"

"When she fell, the knife in her went into me." She pointed under her left breast.

"Oh no!" Raven pulled up her sister's dress and looked. "It's almost healed. Does it hurt?"

"Only a little." Morning Dove pulled her dress down. "Strong Eagle and Jacqo took care of me, and I felt better every day. Then, one morning, I woke thinking I had soiled myself again, but it was something else."

"Oh?" Raven looked up.

"It was my first moon."

"Ooohweee..."

"Jacqo walked me to the bathing hole and helped me." Morning Dove blushed. Raven smiled, looking down as the men tied the last of the leather onto the frame of the teepee, then turned back to her sister. "We went back to the camp, and I went into the moon lodge for three days. I dreamt about Mama. At the end of the dream, I saw you in a circle of women sitting underneath a tree with an old woman. She cackled and waved her arms as she told stories. You were sewing beads onto leather but looked up at me, smiled, and told me to follow the chickadee."

"And the chickadee led you here?"

"Yes," she nodded, "we kept seeing her around, but she always flew south."

"I've seen her as well, almost every day."

"I miss Mama." Morning Dove pulled her knees to her chest and laid her head on them. Her shoulders shook as she wept. "And Chitto." Raven held her sister as she cried, watching Jacqo lead Willie through the trees, taking the mule to the river to drink.

"What about Jacqo?" Raven lifted Morning Dove's chin. "Do you like him?"

"Yes." Morning Dove smiled through her tears. "I feel butterflies in my belly when he is near."

"Have you......?" Raven started, eyes wide, grabbing her sister's hand.

"No." Morning Dove looked away. "I hope he and Andre stay. Do you think they will?"

"I don't know." Raven squeezed her hand. "Sister, there is something I need to tell you."

"What?"

"I carry Strong Eagle's baby." She put her hand over the bulge in her belly.

"I know." Morning Dove shrugged. "We all knew."

Raven stared at her, mouth open.

"We saw you and Strong Eagle go off together. Then at first, your face got round, then your belt got tight. I heard Mama talking to Lone Elk. They were worried about the gossip, hoping you and Strong Eagle would marry soon."

"I didn't think anyone knew." Raven bowed her head, a tear staining her dress. "I'm glad Mama knew. I wish I would have told her sooner." Stopping, she looked up at Morning Dove. "Lone Elk knew?"

"Everyone knew." Morning Dove said. "Will you marry Strong Eagle?"

"Yes." Raven looked away. "Unless he no longer wants me."

"Give him time. He needs rest and food. All he thought about was finding you." Morning Dove paused. "Andre wanted to return to the last village the way they came. But Strong Eagle insisted on going south. He saw the clues you left for him."

"I'd given up. I didn't believe anyone was coming."

Morning Dove jumped up. "Come with me," she called over her shoulder, scrambling down the rocks. Raven followed as Morning Dove hurried over to the things the men had taken off the travois and piled on the ground. She pulled out a large bundle wrapped in rawhide and opened it. Raven knelt next to her, excited to see what it held.

Pulling the last fold of the hide open, Morning Dove revealed Raven's beads and feathers. Neatly tucked underneath was the wedding dress she made for her marriage to Strong Eagle.

Raven burst into tears, large drops falling on the tins of beads, glimmering like dots of silver in the sunlight. She held up her dress, the beaded sun on the chest shining.

"Thank you. Oh, Morning Dove, thank you." She hugged her sister. "I still can't believe you're here."

FIVE

Raven felt a tug on her dress. She turned to see Aponi with Little Wolf close behind. "This is Etu." Aponi held out her doll to Raven.

"Oh, Aponi, she's beautiful. Tell me about her." Aponi looked to Morning Dove for help.

"Our little sister got up early one morning and went exploring." She tousled Aponi's hair. "She went off the path chasing a butterfly and fell into the river."

"It was pretty," Aponi whispered. "I wanted to touch it."

Raven met Morning Dove's eyes. "You went to the river by yourself, Aponi?"

"I was in the moon lodge," Morning Dove said. "Andre saw her leave and followed."

Raven nodded in understanding. "Then what happened?" She sat and listened while Aponi told the story.

"Andre saved me." Aponi finished, brown eyes wide, brimming with tears. "I was scared."

"Yes, I would be too." Raven pulled her sister close. "Promise from now on you'll always go with someone?" Aponi nodded. "Andre gave you Etu?"

"He thought I was lonely without my other doll." Aponi stroked the long purple braid on Etu.

"Ahh, what happened to your other doll?"

"I gave it to Chitto... he was sleeping with Mama." She looked up at Raven. "I hope he likes it."

"I'm sure he does," Raven said.

"I gave her Chitto's bag to carry Etu in," Morning Dove said.

"And this." Aponi held up the bag and pulled out an arrow. "This is from Chitto. He's our Spirit Warrior now."

"Oh, that's wonderful. Chitto dreamed of the day he would be a warrior. Now he is one." Aponi got up and wandered over to where Little Wolf sat in the sun, kneeling in the grass beside him. The pup looked up at her, nuzzling her hand for the jerky he knew would be there.

"Does she remember anything?"

Morning Dove shrugged. "She doesn't talk about it. I see her whispering to Etu. "

"Maybe in time, she'll talk to us."

"She knows Mama and Chitto are asleep in the grave." Morning Dove looked up at Raven. "I kept your things and left Dadas in the teepee. Strong Eagle burned everything else."

Raven looked up. "Do you think Dada will come back?"

"I don't know," Morning Dove said. "I wanted to leave clues, but Strong Eagle wouldn't let me. He said Dada would know how to find us if he returned to the village."

"Strong Eagle is right. If Dada lives...."

SIX

Lusio shuffled along the river, dust flying in circles around his feet. He looked down at his toes, which stuck out of dirty, threadbare moccasins. Stopping, he studied the scattered footprints on the path. Nearby, off to the trail side, there was a pile of dried dung and hoofprints. He picked up the manure and broke it in half.

Still moist. Something was tied here. Recently. Traders? Foes? Friends?

At the riverbank, he knelt, letting the icy water run over his calloused hands, then scooped it up and splashed his face before drinking. Water ran down his arms, making streaks in the grime from weeks on the trail. He longed for the relief of the bathing hole, but restlessness filled him. Following the river back toward the village, he stopped and stared at a lizard sunning himself on a large rock. The lizard stood up on its front legs, chest heaving in and out, and stared back.

"What is your message?" The lizard stared into his eyes, then scrambled down the side of the rock and into a crevice. "I don't understand," Lusio mumbled.

Back in camp, Lusio stared at the two teepees left standing. The one he shared with Aiyani and their children was closed tight. Desperate to know, with trembling fingers, he reached out to untie the lace. As his hand met the leather, hardened from repeated use, visions of what he might find inside terrified him. Dropping his hand, he turned and walked away.

A small campsite sat between the two teepees, the other Lone Elks. Inside, the teepee Strong Eagle shared with his father was swept clean, yet a scent of infection lingered. He dug where the cache of food had been buried. Anything of value was gone. Wandering back to his teepee, he stood staring at the door. The need to know outweighed his fear, and hands shaking, he untied the leather thong holding the door shut. Pulling the flap back, he stepped in. A heady scent of lavender filled the space. Inhaling deeply, Lusio felt the energy in his legs and feet open and root deep into the earth, calming him. Aiyani, she taught him how to do this.

Their teepee was always full of herbs and plants that Aiyani gathered to make medicines. Memories and smells pulled him into a daydream, tempting him to lie down and become lost. But shaking his head, he focused. Except for a neatly stacked pile of clothing straight ahead of him, the teepee was empty.

Sitting cross-legged on the ground, he went through the pile. Someone saved his things. He lay his clothing to the side and unwrapped the sleeping fur, placing it where he and Aiyani slept. As he unrolled it, a heavy object fell out, bouncing off his knee. He recognized the handle of the knife, a carved image of a large bird. Strong Eagle was well known for his art. *Strong Eagle, he lives?*

Gratitude filled him as he unrolled the rest of the fur. Tucked deep inside was a pouch of dried meat and fruit. His mouth watered as he reached for a piece of jerky, then looked up, noticing a skin of water leaning against the back of the teepee. Filled with the love and care he thought lost, Lusio ate and drank. It had been days since he stopped to hunt or fish. As his belly filled, he wondered whose hands prepared this. Were they with spirit now? Wrapped in the fur and exhausted after weeks of walking, he slept, dreams riddled with memories of being beaten and tortured by the soldiers. Pain in his ankle woke him as the afternoon waned. Gathering his things, Lusio set off to the bathing hole.

Dropping his dirty clothes on the ground, he stepped in. The morning sun sparkled on the icy water as he floated, feeling the grime float away, replaced with the relief of being in familiar surroundings. Eyes closed, he could hear the playful splash of water as Chitto and Aponi played nearby. Drifting, he imagined the soft murmurs from Aiyani, Morning Dove, and Raven, their chatter lighthearted as they washed each other's hair. A scent of pine and lavender swirled around him. Smiling, he opened his eyes and looked over, expecting to see his family. But all he saw were the gentle waves made from the movement of his arms. He was alone.

Many years ago, when he first stepped into this village, he didn't expect to find the joy and love he realized with this tribe. He had strived to be a good man because of them.

Sitting on the riverbank, the heat from the morning sun dried him. Scooping handfuls of clay from the water's edge, he packed it around his injured ankle. The mud tightened as it dried. Ripping a strip of leather off his old shirt, he wrapped it around his ankle. Dressing, the soft leather of clean leggings and shirt felt good on his skin. He sat watching the steady flow of the river. Who saved my things?

Wandering back to camp, Lusio dug through the ashes of the community fire pit. On the outer edge was the remnant of a walking stick. Picking it up, his heart sank as he brushed it off and saw the familiar carvings.   One of the first things he noticed about Aiyani so many years ago was her strength, despite her limp. He wanted to gift her something to help her as she climbed the hills and mesas, gathering herbs and plants. His fingers traced the spiral shapes he carved on the walking stick, now a burnt piece of wood. Hair falling on his face stuck to the tears rolling down his cheeks. Pulling a red cloth out of the pouch on his hip, he combed his hair back with his fingers, wiped his face, then wrapped the bandana around his forehead, knotting it on the side.

It's my fault. I should have been here. Defying the custom to not keep items of the dead, lest their Spirit is held earthbound, Lusio put the charred wood in his pouch. What if I'm wrong? Maybe she lives. A pinecone fell from the tree above, glancing off his shoulder. He looked up. The chickadee perched on a pine bough, the branch gently bouncing. The bird became still and stared into his eyes, then fluttered its wings before flying off. Something about it brought a lightness into his heart.

Lusio spent the day tracing footprints and studying paths leading in and out of the village. He found large moccasin prints alongside the bare footprints of a child. Then another of a young person, a female by the slender shape of the foot. Lusio spent the day tracing footsteps, studying paths leading in and out of the village. Other prints were a combination of moccasins and boots, plus hoofprints.

Two traders, a mule, and three survivors?

Under the shade of the trees by the back campsite, he found more dung, softer than he'd seen earlier on the river trail. Impressions in the grass where someone slept surrounded it. The fire was cold, but fresh grease stains on the flat rocks showed something had been cooked recently. He saw tracks and signs that something had been drug on the southern trail leading out of the camp along the river. He would go that way first. But the pain in his ankle reminded him of the need to rest.

As the sky grew dark, he built a fire and cooked three freshly caught, gutted, and cleaned perch. He devoured the food, adding wild lettuce and berries collected throughout the day. Then, unable to sleep, with the path lit by moonlight, he went and sat on the center stone of the Sacred Circle, which covered the gravesite. He called out to his grandfather, whom he adored as a child, and prayed for help.

Much like Chitto, Lusio had been a happy boy growing up in his southern Pueblo tribe on the Zuni River. He and his friends climbed the tall sandstone mesas, finding footholds or making narrow stairways in places unseen by the ordinary eye. Every family had a home atop Corn Mountain, which was a refuge when attacked by invading tribes or the Spaniards. Still, much of their everyday life was down on the pueblo. Long days of sunshine and abundant water from the nearby river made the land fertile, where they grew corn, squash, and beans. Afternoons were spent on the riverbank fashioning pottery for the ovens.

In the summers, it was his job to escort his mother to the top of the mesa. She would dig up a particular type of sandstone on the west side of the mountain, used to create the flat stones they cooked Do'he'we, a thin, flaky cornmeal paste bread, an art passed down by their elders. The sandstone was prepared by smoothing and shaping it, then seasoned by rubbing pinon gum and pumpkin seeds, covering every inch of the stone before placing it over a fire. It could take all day, as the stone needed to be hot enough for the gum and seeds to melt and be absorbed by the stone. Most importantly, one needed to prepare it with positive thoughts and feelings, so good things would come to those who ate the bread. A mystical art, one few women excelled at, required patience and deep meditation. Once a woman acquired the craft, it often led to a prestigious offer of marriage, which was how Lusio's mother came to marry the chief's son. But no one foresaw the changes coming.

Old stories said lingering spirits, unsuccessful in their journey to the afterlife, attached themselves to unwitting men, women, and children. As they were known, witches had been a part of their culture from their earliest memories. The council of Priests studied the tribe for signs of witchcraft, creating constant fear among the people. When illness, droughts, or floods came, the council determined who among them was to blame for the misfortune. The accused hung by their wrists from the rocks, feet inches off the ground until they confessed, and chased from the tribe, banished for life.

Lusio, jovial on the outside, confidently walked around the camp, helping his grandfather, their chief. Assuming he would one day succeed Nana, he watched everyone closely, never revealing the worry that lay deep inside. His mother, whom everyone called Hotda, was a healer sought after by many.

"Quick... get Hotda...." were frequently heard in the village. He smiled at the memory.

After the death of her husband, Hotda often stayed on the outskirts of the tribe, happier in nature. But things were changing, and the council of Priests, desperate to maintain control amidst a dwindling tribe, had other ideas. He'd seen them watch his mother out of the corner of their eye, which worried him. Lusio loved his mother. The thought of her delicate wrists being bound, hanging from the rock ledge, was more than he could bear. After his grandfather's mysterious death, which Hotda could not cure, a drought came. Lusio saw the High Priests gather in council in intense discussion. When they came for his mother, he stepped out in front of her. "It was me. Take me."

"No, Lusio." His mother sobbed. "No."

Stomach churning with fear, he looked at his mother, knowing she wouldn't survive banishment. Once accused of being a witch, the person becomes dead to the tribe, not allowed to return. He watched as his sister, Lolotea, took their mother and faded into a group of women and girls.

Lusio hung from the rock for two days, then was cut down and chased from the village. He found a bow, arrows, an extra set of moccasins, a waterskin, and his knife in a pile on the outskirts. Afraid to return and bring greater harm to his mother and sister, he left and traveled north, never hearing what happened to his people. Traversing the land, he used his skills as a tracker and hunter to survive, always grateful to see the sunrise each day. Friendly and unassuming, he wove his way through soldiers, missionaries, and mountain men, trading his skills for tools and other things he needed to survive. He hunted and tanned leather for clothing. Occasionally, he would scout for the Apache, but after warning the vulnerable tribe of an oncoming attack, he slipped into the night, disappearing before the Apache realized he wasn't their ally.

The absence of his mother and the love of family and a village to call his own haunted him. He didn't know how long he wandered, but the day he walked into Lone Elk's camp, an instant friendship formed when the two men's eyes met and their hands locked in a handshake. The next day, he watched from afar as Aiyani dipped a pitcher into the river for water. As she stood, he noticed her small, stout build and the slight limp she walked with. Lusio stepped out from behind the trees and offered to carry the water for her. She smiled, amusement in her eyes. The morning walk from the river to the main camp became a daily routine with natural ease between them. Over time, the tribe accepted him, and Lusio found the love lost when he was banished from his childhood village.

Much time had passed since he left with the traders. Sitting on the Center Stone of the Sacred Circle now, he could feel the energy of bodies resting under the soil as their spirits soared. The evening breeze softly caressed his neck, and a scent of lavender whirled around him. Startled, he pushed himself up off the stone and looked around. "Aiyani?"

Lusio walked to the south stone of the Sacred Circle, longing for comfort. He'd never felt so alone. "It's like you're here with me, yet when I look... you're not there." Lusio looked to the stars for answers. "I'm sorry, Aiyani," he whispered. "I failed you. I failed our children. I didn't mean to...." He nested his face in his hands as guilt flooded him. In the stunned silence of grief, he walked to the west stone, kneeling with his head pressed down on the ground.

"The soldiers were waiting for us on the other side of the mountain." He spoke aloud as if someone were listening. "They killed the traders and took all their things. Then they beat me. I thought I would die there, but I woke as water was splashed on my face and a rope was tied around me. Days and nights ran into each other as we traveled, with little to eat or drink. The further south we went, I began to recognize the mesas of my childhood. One night, the guard wandered away, and I got the rope off. Pulling myself to the ravine's edge, I rolled down into the cacti and mesquite bushes."

Lusio lay himself down on the ground and continued in a whisper. "They took my knife, so for two days, hiding while they looked for me, I used a sharp stick to get water out of a cactus. Eventually, they gave up and left." Sitting up, he pulled the scarf off his head, nervously running his fingers through his hair. "The world spun when I stood, and my ankle buckled after walking a short way. I could see the fringe of my old village in the distance. Somehow, I made it to Corn Mountain, found one of the hidden staircases, and crawled to the top." Arms wrapped around his knees, he bounced his head softly on them and groaned. "When I woke, I lay in a hut on soft skins. My sister Lolotea kneeled beside me, washing my face with cool water. I thought I was dead and we were on our next journey together. I never thought I would see her again." Lusio stretched out his legs and rubbed his sore ankle.

"I drifted in and out of a stupor for days. When I woke, Lolotea told me of my mother's heartbreak when I took her punishment and was chased from the village. She said afterward Hotda spent most of her days in nature, rarely talking to people, only returning when someone needed healing. Over time, Hotda became blind but still navigated the outer world easily. I thought my mother was dead, but the next day, Lolotea entered, leading Hotda to me. My mother sat next to me. She just held my hand and sponged the fevered sweat off my forehead, murmuring my name. I slept. When I woke, she was gone."

Rising, Lusio walked to the north stone of the Sacred Circle and looked up as a shooting star streaked across the sky. "I don't know how many days and nights I lay there, drifting in and out of a fevered sleep. One morning, I woke to find a woman curled next to me. We were naked under the blankets. She sat up, smiled at me, and brushed the hair out of my eyes. Then she rose, dressed, and left the hut. I never saw her again." Lusio sat in silence.

"I'm sorry, Aiyani. I didn't act with honor and instead became lost in a dream. But while I was lost, the soldiers came here. I should have been here. With you. With my family." Restless, Lusio picked up the waterskin, drained it, and threw it aside. "Soon after, my ankle healed enough to travel, and I returned. But I was too late." He spat on the ground. "I will find who is left. I pray it's you."

Circling back to the center stone, he heard the howl of a pack of coyotes in the distance and looked up at a moon almost full. "I must go... soon."

SEVEN

The night grew cold as the group sat silently around the fire. Raven stood. "It's late. We must rest." She smiled down at Strong Eagle, taking his hand as he stood. "You haven't seen my cave. Come, I have a surprise for you."

Raven turned to a touch on her shoulder and pulled Morning Dove into a hug. Andre picked up Aponi, who'd fallen asleep leaning against his knee. As he ducked to go into the teepee, Raven stopped him. "Thank you, Andre." She stroked Aponi's hair, then leaned in, kissing her forehead. Aponi woke briefly at Raven's kiss, smiled, and lay her head back on Andre's shoulder. As he bent and stepped in, Morning Dove held the cloth door open, careful not to disturb Aponi. He lay her down, pulling the soft, rabbit fur blanket Raven left in the teepee over her, then tucked the bag with Etu next to her so she would see it first thing when she woke.

Jacqo stood near the fire, looking up as Morning Dove dropped the flap. She smiled at him, then blushed as she saw the grin on Raven and Strong Eagle's faces.

"We'll make sweet tea in the morning," Raven said. "Just like we used to." Taking Strong Eagle's hand, she led him across the clearing towards the stones, passing Willie, who snorted as he grazed on the grass near the chokecherry bushes. At the cave entrance sat Little Wolf, hair bristling as he looked at Strong Eagle.

"Wait here." Raven went into the cave, returning with dried rabbit meat from the food cache. Little Wolf's nose quivered at the scent of the meat. She handed it to Strong Eagle, nodding towards the pup. He took it and breaking off a piece, put it in the palm of his hand and held it out. Little Wolf took it eagerly, then sat in anticipation of the rest. Shaking his head, he tossed the rest of the scraps to the pup. Satisfied, Little Wolf trotted down the rocks toward the camp. Halfway down, he stopped, his ears perking up at the sound of howling in the distance, then looked up at Raven.

"Is that your family, Little Wolf?" Raven called softly.

Strong Eagle looked at Raven and then the pup, surprised at the bond the two had formed.

"One night, I woke to find him under the sleeping fur, curled by my side. At first, I thought it was Chitto, but once I woke fully, I realized it wasn't." She took a deep breath, watching Little Wolf as he scrambled down the rocks, then trot through the meadow and trees, out of sight. "At night, I heard them howl. It scared me... I couldn't defend myself from the whole pack. But then I found his mother dead."

Raven turned as he stepped into the cave, silently looking at everything she had gathered. He ran his fingers over the wolf hide leaning against the cave wall, then picked up two pieces of wood, tossing them onto the fire. "Perhaps they were calling him."

"I tried to make him go away, but he wouldn't leave. Then one day, as his eyes began changing from blue to brown, I saw your father's eyes. I felt safe, surrounded by those I loved, even though I believed everyone was dead. Oh, Strong Eagle, Lone Elk." She reached down and touched the knife in the sheath on his hip. "What happened?"

Strong Eagle stepped onto the ledge and stared at the stars glimmering above them. "I found him in the woods behind the big fire pit. He was laying on top of Aponi with an arrow in his back."

Raven gasped and took his arm.

"He saved her... she was barely breathing when I found them." He sat down heavily on the rock ledge. Raven got the sleeping fur from the cave and wrapped it around him. "My sleeping fur," he muttered, running his fingers over it.

"Yes. When I saw the men in our camp, I ran into your teepee. I grabbed the bundle and your sleeping fur. Then I heard the men." Raven reached into the pocket under her belt, touching the talisman, wishing her mother were there. Strong Eagle looked over at her face, wet with tears, and opened the fur, inviting her in. Raven huddled up against him. "I heard them trying to untie the front flap of the teepee. I was scared and ran out the back."

They sat in silence for moments, wrapped together in the fur.

"Had we not gone to the rocks, I would have been guarding the village entrance. Instead, I let Running Elk go." Strong Eagle pulled up his knees and lay his head on them, voice muffled. "I tried to get to him, but it was too late. He died fighting like the warrior he always dreamed of being. The warrior he was."

"Running Elk..." Raven sighed.

"It should have been me, not him. I'm no warrior." Strong Eagle turned his head, waving his hand towards the inside of the cave, then turned back to her. "Look at all you've done. Perhaps a woman doesn't need a man to survive. Perhaps you don't need me. I don't know what to think or what to feel anymore."   "Strong Eagle, no."

"Bad spirits try to come for me. I push them away, but they're always close, waiting for me to fall asleep so they can come into my dreams. They tell me what a weak man I am, or no man at all." He looked up as a star shot across the sky. "But then I hear my father's voice."

Raven looked up. "What does he say?"

"It's up to you now, son... that's what he says." Strong Eagle shook his head as if to clear thoughts away. "Yet I did nothing but lay wounded in a ravine, unable to save myself. I've failed everyone I loved."

"You saved my sisters," Raven whispered. "And you're here for me now."

Strong Eagle sighed and shook off the fur, standing.

Raven reached up to him. "When you didn't come to the rocks, I went back to the village in the morning. Dead bodies lay scattered on the ground. The smell... I retched." She started to sob. "They were my friends, my family. I started to go to them, but those men came out of the woods. Running away, I tripped over my mother's arm and fell. I knew she was dead, yet my body was frozen. Then I heard her voice telling me to get away. It was the last time I saw my mother."

"Stop, Raven. Just stop. Please."

"No." Her voice raised to a loud whisper as she looked up at him. "Maybe I don't deserve happiness or joy either. Maybe the pleasure we had with each other denies us. But our baby doesn't deserve to suffer. I had to feed her, feed us. I had to plan. I thought you were dead." She turned away, face in her hands, sobbing. "I didn't even return to find out. Every day I took steps back to our village, but the voices of those men, laughing, with drool running down their faces, filled my head. I couldn't."

Strong Eagle sat staring stonily into the night for a moment, then turned, his face softening as he saw her anguish. "I'm sorry."

Raven touched his face. "How did Andre and Jacqo find you? Were the soldiers in the village still there?"

He shrugged. "I don't remember much. Fighting, falling down the ravine. A heavy branch had fallen over my legs, pinning me down. They pulled me out."

"And the soldiers?"

"Andre and Jacqo put me in a clearing, then left to check the village. While I lay there, I had a vision. My parents were with me. My mother kissed me on the cheek." He looked over at her. "All I ever wanted was to know my mother. I wanted to sleep in her arms and be held like a baby, stay that way forever. I tried, but I woke. Looking up at the sway of a tree branch, I saw a chickadee perched on it. It was then I knew my father was dead as well. I stumbled out to the village. Andre was pinned under a soldier's knee, and Jacqo was rolling towards the firepit with another. I picked up the musket and shot the soldier. Andre jumped up and tackled the other soldier who was about to slit Jacqo's throat, slitting the soldier's throat instead. And then there were no more soldiers left alive."

"So you saved Andre and Jacqo?"

"Yes." He looked at her. "The next day, Jacqo found Morning Dove, and I found Aponi." He hung his head. "We did our best to honor the dead. Andre and Jacqo dug a grave, and we gave the dead gifts to help them on their journey. Then I built a Sacred Circle over the top."

"You did well, Strong Eagle. I'm sorry I wasn't there for you. For our people."

He leaned in and wrapped his arms around her. "Do you want to go back? Their spirits have flown, but you could see where their bodies lay."

"No, it would do no good. I should have been there to help you. To bury my mother."

"You took care of our baby. We're together now."

"Every day, I prayed someone would come." Raven cradled her head on his shoulder. "And when no one did, I started back. But those awful men... I couldn't. I was afraid."

"You did the right thing."

"I remembered everything you taught me and called on my father's spirit." She touched his forehead with hers and whispered: "It's good to know I can do this, yet I don't wish to do it alone. I choose you as my mate and the father of my children." She caressed his face. "I choose you as my lover and my best friend. Always." Holding his face in her hands, she kissed him. "Come. Let's rest." Taking his hand, she led him inside the cave. His heart melted watching the grace of her as she spread his sleeping fur. Raven reached out as he knelt next to her, stroking the white feather braided into his hair, the stem wrapped with her hair. "You found it."

"It gave me hope when I had none." Raven pulled him to her and kissed him.

Jacqo sat near the fire, watching as everyone settled for the night. Morning Dove stepped into the teepee, and as she reached up to pull the cloth door shut, she looked out, caught Jacqo's gaze, held it for a moment, and then pulled the door down. Stoking the small fire in the center of the teepee, she checked on Aponi and then turned to unroll her sleeping fur. On impulse, Morning Dove picked up the fur, wrapped it around her shoulders, turned, and pushed the flap open. Outside, she looked up at the stars in the clear night sky. "Do you think Mama and Chitto are watching over us?" She asked, walking over to him.

"Oui."

Sitting down, she opened the blanket so it hung loosely around them. Jacqo reached down to take her hand as she lay her head on his shoulder. They sat quietly as shapes formed in the fire and then disappeared, light flickering on their faces.

Andre lay on his blanket, seeing the romance blossom before him. Once across the mountains, he wanted to head east to where other Huguenots had settled. The land was free to those who wanted to stay. Pulling his mother's cross from his pocket, he traced the pattern, picturing her face. He wanted to find his people, have a home and a community. Hoped to take them all there and make a fresh start.

Would they come? As a star streaked across the sky, doubt crept into his heart. Minutes later, sleep claimed him, riddled with dreams of his boyhood in France... one moment happy as their family recited prayers around the dinner table, only to be interrupted by a loud banging on the door.

EIGHT

Lusio woke with a start.

Coyotes... Dreaming?

The howling came again.

Not dreaming...

Reaching down, he felt comfort at the touch of his knife. It was the only weapon he had. Unable to sleep, he went out to the small camp and stirred the fire. Warming himself, he watched the flickers of faces and images as the fire danced. In the distance, as the howl of the coyotes came again, he remembered those same sounds as a boy.

"What are they telling us, Nana?" Lusio would ask his grandfather.

"Ah K'yasse," Nana said to the small boy. "The Suski, they have much to teach us."

"But Nana," Lusio insisted. "I thought they were tricksters."

His grandfather chuckled. "Yes, just like us. Sometimes they trick even themselves. Suski teaches us all things are sacred, yet nothing is sacred. You'll understand one day."

"Do they mean us harm, Nana?" Lusio asked, sitting over a steaming bowl of corn mush. "Will they come into our camp?"

"No, K'yasse," his grandfather responded. "They sing us into being, reminding us of our true nature. They teach us to be humble. Great Spirit asks us to be honest and true. Suski teaches us this."

Lusio pondered the memory as the howling grew distant. Climbing the steep path to the mesa, he watched his feet disappear in the dense, early morning fog. A scent of lavender led him to the nearest bush. After gathering an armful of the fragrant branches, he stopped to breathe, letting the plant's essence fill him.

Aiyani...

The buds of the lavender were closed tight, waiting for the light of day to open. As he walked back into the village, Lusio allowed the voices and chatter of the tribe who had accepted and loved him all these years to flow through his body, imprinting his soul. It was as if he were a cloth being woven, the pattern ever-changing. His body would cease to exist at some point in this lifetime. Still, the pattern would continue evolving as his soul journeyed through other lifetimes. Stepping onto the gravesite, he lay the lavender on the center stone of the Sacred Circle, certain in his heart that Aiyani lay there.

Lame from his injured ankle, his shuffling gait left streaks in the dirt as he walked over and stood on the round, flat stone marking the north on the Sacred Circle. It was the place of winter, of buffalo, where life challenges you to be a warrior. He didn't feel like a warrior and wasn't sure how many battles were left in him. He was tired. Beaten. As he stepped off the stone, his ankle gave out, and he fell in a heap on the ground, crying out in pain. Grief came in overwhelming waves as the disappointments of his life threatened to dominate his spirit. He lay, letting the energy of the earth soothe him. Placing his palms on the ground, he pushed himself up.

Retracing his steps, he moved towards the cornerstone of the south, craving the comfort of the laughter and innocence of children. His children. Chitto's laughter. He could feel it reach up from the earth and fill him. He wanted his son. Tears dropped heavy on the ground as he walked the wheel, feeling the rivers of his life flow through him. That same river continually flowed in his blood, cleansing that which was hurt and wounded. He reached the smooth, red claystone that marked the south. Standing on it, he turned to face the north. The battles he fought weighed heavy in his bones, yet resting at the south stone, he could feel the healing energy rise through his feet from the earth.

At the center stone, a shape swirled up through the mist of the morning fog, revealing the back of a man wrapped in a ceremonial robe. The figure turned to walk towards the west, where all beings cross in their final journey from this life.

"No," Lusio cried. "No. Come back!"

The figure turned and faced him. It was Lone Elk. Lusio could still feel the strength of Lone Elk's handshake and the instant friendship formed when they met so long ago. He felt the chief's energy spiral through the mist and into his heart, connecting with the energy moving through his legs like a healing salve. Then the figure swirled back into the mist and was gone. As the fog began to lift, his tiredness washed away. Lusio crossed the Sacred Circle to the east stone with a lighter step. Kneeling, he kissed the earth, resting his forehead on the dirt mound covering the dead, feeling strength from those he loved. Holding his hands to the rising sun, he gave thanks to the promise of new beginnings. A short distance away, rustling in the bushes made him look. He stood and turned as a coyote passed, crossing from the north to the south. It stopped and looked into his eyes, then trotted into the grass. Lusio now understood what the coyote was telling him on the last morning of his journey home. Suski had been warning him of the loss and devastation he would face if he continued. Had I turned around, I would have never known what happened. *How would that have helped? Is this my new beginning?*

But today, the coyote traveled south. As Lusio stood and watched, he could still hear the shrill voice of the storyteller of his youth: "If Suski crosses to the south, you will have good luck and healing. But you must always pray with joy for this, even if you don't know what will come. Suski asks you to trust Great Spirit." Perhaps Lone Elk had prayed and appeased the spirits after all.

He looked up as the sun broke through the clouds, marveling at the chickadee who hovered above him before flying into the trees. Lusio walked to the Center Stone. Leaning down, he broke off a sprig of lavender and blew softly into the buds. "Thank you, Great Spirit, for the message of the coyote. For showing me the way." He pulled the buds off the lavender and sprinkled them around the center stone. "I will find whoever is left. I promise." Stepping out of the Sacred Circle, he stood and looked one last time at the mound of earth covering those who died here.

For the second time, Lusio set off to cross the mountains on a trek he didn't expect to make. He looked at his pack. Meager, but more than he'd come with. His ankle was packed in mud and wrapped snugly in a strip of leather. After taking apart the remaining teepees, he cut strips to take with him to bind his ankle. He looked around at the land which had been his home. Cleared, all evidence a village once existed here had been erased. It was time for this piece of earth to reclaim herself.

As he took his first step away from the old village, chatter from the tree above him caught his attention. The yellow-bellied chickadee sang a morning song. Wings fluttering, she took flight, circling Lusio three times before flying away, south along the river. A tiny spark of joy ignited in Lusio's heart.

NINE

Strong Eagle woke as the first hint of morning light sparkled against the cave walls. His hand cradled Raven's swollen belly, ripe with hope for their future. *My child. Our child.*

Pulling his hand back, he perched himself up on his elbow, gazing down at Raven, her hair spread across the fur, face peaceful. *So beautiful.*

He rolled out from under the sleeping fur, careful not to wake her. On his way down the rocks, he saw Little Wolf watching him from the trees. Gazing into the pup's eyes. he could see that Raven was right. It was Lone Elk's thoughtful gaze. "Thank you, father, for sending this little pup to her."

Andre watched the interaction with Little Wolf out of the corner of his eye, curious as Strong Eagle disappeared down the path leading out of the clearing and towards the old village.

Following the path back to the puma, Strong Eagle stepped into the brush and pulled out the dead animal's remains. Removing the pouch of corn pollen, he offered a pinch to the north trail leading back to the old village and another to the fork in the path leading south. He then retraced his steps back to the puma, where his old life and new had come together. Sprinkling corn pollen around the big cat, he prayed:

> *"My tribe whose spirits travel elsewhere,*
> *I carry you in my heart.*
> *I will honor you with every step I take.*
> *Humbly, I ask for your blessing.*
> *Please, Great Spirit, guide us as we leave this place.*
> *Bring light to our path and open our long eyes,*
> *that we might recognize it."*

Andre stood in the shadows, watching as Strong Eagle dropped to his knees, pulling the head of the puma to him, and said:

> *"Thank you for this animal, for her sacrifice,*
> *that Raven and I live and are reunited.*
> *We will honor the Spirit of Puma always."*

Pulling out the knife he received from his father, Strong Eagle struggled to remove the two long, pointed teeth from the jaw of the large animal. As the head, stiffened in death, rolled out of his grip, he sighed in frustration, then looked up in surprise at Andre, who knelt next to his friend, holding the head of the puma steady.

Strong Eagle nodded in gratitude as he used his knife to remove the teeth. "Big medicine," he said. "It brings the blessings of those who now walk with Spirit and will protect us on our journey ahead." Brushing the teeth clean with damp blades of grass, Strong Eagle placed them in his pouch, then looked up at Andre. "Your mother and father, you miss?"

"Every day, Strong Eagle."

"What happened?"

"They were killed when we were young." Andre's eyes watered. "Jacqo and I left France soon after, which is how we became traders and met you."

"We are blessed to know you. The spirit of your mother and father will live in your heart always." He gathered the remains of the puma, placing it in a nest of grass nearby.

Raven woke, smiling at the scent of her mate mingled in the fur, but reaching down, she only felt the familiar bundle of the pup. "Little Wolf? Was it a dream? Did no one come?" He stretched, then scampered away as she jumped up. Heart racing, she stood and rushed out to the ledge. Relief ran through her as she looked down and saw her sisters pouring sweet tea into the pottery cups they had brought from the village. They looked up and smiled. With Little Wolf at her heels, Raven climbed down the rocks, reaching the fire just as Strong Eagle and Andre walked into the clearing. Hands shaking, she accepted a cup of tea from Morning Dove and then, with her heart pounding, walked over and met Strong Eagle halfway across. "I woke, and you were gone."

Folding her into his arms, he pulled her face up with his fingertips. "Never will I leave you again." Raven sobbed into his shoulder, releasing the fear and grief which had haunted her since the massacre. When she looked up, he brushed the hair from her cheeks. "Will you be my mate, marry me today?"

Raven studied his face. His eyes were clear, and the vacant look was gone. "Yes," She said, eyes glittering with tears. "As the sun leaves the sky tonight?"

"Let's tell them."

"Raven and I will marry tonight, at sunset," Strong Eagle announced as they joined the group at the fire. Morning Dove and Aponi squealed joyfully and ran over, hugging their sister. Andre reached out and shook Strong Eagle's hand, then Jacqo grinned, pulling him into a hug.

Raven sat on the grass in the clearing with the basket on her lap. Pulling out her wedding dress, she held it to her breast and smiled at her sister. "Yesterday, I woke alone, and no one had come. I was prepared to leave, hoping to find a village to take me in." She looked down, running her fingers over the sun she beaded on the dress, then reached over and took Morning Dove's hand. "I feel as if I'm dreaming. But you're real. And soon, I'll be Strong Eagle's mate."

"Let's go to the river. We'll wash your hair." Morning Dove pulled yucca root out of a pack on the travois. "And pick fresh berries and flowers to put in your hair, as Mama would do."

Aponi came running out of the trees, Little Wolf on her heels. Laughing, Raven called, "Come to the river with us? You and Etu can help me get ready."

At the bathing hole, they undressed and stepped into the water, scattering the tiny fish swimming just under the surface.

"Little Wolf!" Morning Dove cried as he jumped in, splashing them. Aponi giggled.

Raven smiled as the soft sounds of her sisters filled her. "You bring joy to my heart." She hugged them. "You too, Little Wolf," laughing as he nosed into the group. Sitting on the bank, Morning Dove combed Raven's hair with her fingers until the tangles were out, and her hair lay like silk on her back.

A breeze rose as the late afternoon sun moved through the trees. Strong Eagle cleaned and polished the two long, pointed teeth he retrieved from the puma, carefully etching a hole through the top of each one. He strung narrow strips of leather through the holes, then held the necklaces up. The angles of each tooth, uniquely similar but different, lit up as the sun shone through the tree's branches above, creating long, sharp shadows on the ground. Ignoring the painful reality of the shadows in his own soul, he opened the pouch and sprinkled corn pollen on them, asking spirit to bless their union.

"Strong Eagle," Jacqo called, motioning him over.

Brushing off his buckskin pants and shirt, he joined the brothers. Andre held up four strips of colored cloth in his hands.

"Handfasting," Jacqo said. "We saw it at an English settlement where there wasn't a holy man." Jacqo held out his hand as Andre demonstrated.

"Ah." Strong Eagle looked at Andre. "Rope ceremony. Will you do?"

"Yes," Andre started, then looked up. Tenderness filled his eyes as he saw Aponi emerge from the path leading from the creek, holding Raven's hand. Seeing Andre's face soften into a smile, Jacqo and Strong Eagle turned to see. Morning Dove stepped out behind Raven, holding her other hand. She looked up and met Jacqo's gaze.

As Raven stepped out of the trees, Strong Eagle felt like his heart might stop. Yellow and purple flowers were woven into her hair, which glistened in the breeze as it fell around her hips. The white leather dress fell gently around her calves as the light caught the beaded sun over her chest, making it shimmer in tendrils that reached out and spiraled into his heart. His eyes filled as wounds began to heal, his breath catching as she walked barefoot across the meadow towards him, each step leaving a soft impression on the grass. Smiling as she grew closer, Raven looked up at him.

Suddenly, trees and bushes rustled as a shape rushed out, water from the creek spraying the girls. "Little Wolf!" the sisters gasped. The men chuckled. Tongue hanging out of the side of his mouth, Little Wolf sat, water dripping off his snout, and looked expectantly at the girls. Aponi reached into her pouch and took a piece of jerky, holding it out to him. Nuzzling her hand, he took it, then went and lay under a tall pine. None saw the chickadee swoop in low, perching on an overhanging branch. A pinecone dropped to the ground, rolling to the feet of Little Wolf, who nudged the cone with his nose, then lay his head between his paws.

The sisters stepped back as Raven turned to face Strong Eagle, her eyes solemn and searching.

Strong Eagle gazed at her, lost in her beauty as the dark shadows inside filled with light.

Jacqo came forward and took their hands, laying one on top of the other. Wrapping the ribbons around their thumbs, Andre bound their hands together. Strong Eagle and Raven turned in a full circle, gazing into each other's eyes.

Strong Eagle began. "Raven, as Grandfather Sun leaves the sky and Grandmother Moon rises, I ask you to be my wife. I want to walk by your side forever, warm you when you're cold, and be your shelter. I will celebrate life with you and with our children. You are my heart and soul, my strength. I wish to be your husband. Will you have me?"

Raven looked up, eyes moist. "Strong Eagle, from my earliest memory, you have been my best friend. I thought I was forever alone one day ago, but now, here you stand. You are my heart. Whether together or apart, every step I take is entwined with yours. I will laugh with you and hold you in your sorrow. I will celebrate life by bearing your children and always walk by your side. Yes, I will be your wife."

The couple turned another full circle, eyes locked. Andre stepped in and untied their hands, folding the strips of cloth, then handed them to Raven. She turned, putting the cloth into Morning Dove's hands, and squeezing her fingers, gave her sister a knowing smile. Morning Dove looked at Jacqo, blushing at his grin.

Raven turned back to Strong Eagle as he reached into his pouch and pulled out the necklaces. Lifting her hair, he draped one around her neck, watching as the tooth of the puma fell between her breasts. Putting the other over his head, he let it hang down his chest. "The spirit of puma gifts us. May we always honor her." Reaching out, he caressed Raven's face, then pulled her into a kiss.

Aponi and Morning Dove came forward and wrapped their arms around the couple, nestling their faces against their backs. Jacqo joined them, but Andre stood back. His stomach tightened with jealousy at the obvious bond formed between his brother and the remaining members of the tribe. Uncertain of their destiny, he stepped in and placed his hands on Jacqo's and Strong Eagle's shoulders.

TEN

Lusio lay restless under the stars in the black of night, drifting in and out of dreams. In one, he was a young boy, happy, running up and down the mesas with his friends, helping his mother as she gathered plants and herbs up on Corn Mountain. Then in the next dream, everything changed, and he was alone. Waking, he looked up at the stars, remembering the day he found Lone Elk and his tribe. After months of surviving on his own, he'd again been blessed with the happiness and joy of a village that accepted him. Watching stars streak across the sky, he wondered who survived and who now were amongst the stars above him. Drifting back into another restless dream, something in the brush moved. In an instant, he was standing in a crouch, knife in hand.

A family of foxes crossed the path, the mother chattering to her young. Lusio berated himself for the fear which sat in his belly like a heavy rock. He curled back up in his blanket, hoping for the escape of sleep, but anxious thoughts whirled in his head like a spider spinning a web. Soon morning would come, and the clear, crisp night sky would be shrouded in fog. Eager to see what lay ahead, he sat up in the dark, wrapped his ankle, then pulled on his moccasins. Pack on his back, with the moon lighting his way, Lusio followed the trail south. Bullfrogs and crickets in the tall grass greeted him with their night songs as he passed. As the clear night sky gave way to early morning fog, each step heavy with fatigue, Lusio stopped to rest. Leaning against a tree, sunlight filtered through the leaves, casting shadows on his face. Falling into a deep sleep, he dreamt of Aiyani and their children. In his dream, Chitto's laughter filled the air with joy.

Awake again, he wondered if any of his children lived. Above him, a skinny branch bounced as the chickadee landed. "You're quite the traveler." He shaded his eyes with his hand and looked up. "Do you have a message for me?" The bird sat still for a moment, then flew higher into the tree, disappearing, only to return a moment later, circling him three times before flying south along the river.

Strong Eagle stood on the edge of the rocks as the drizzle of early morning rain fell. Reluctantly, he had left the warm fur where Raven still slept. Andre stepped into the trees, and Jacqo turned in his bedroll on the grassy area below. The door to the teepee opened and Aponi stuck her head out. She looked up at him, her smile filling his heart with gratitude. This was a good place. They could stay here, but Raven insisted on going south. She wanted to find her father's people. Will they accept us?

Andre wanted them to go east, where people from his homeland settled. "Start fresh, settle down," he argued. Thoughts rumbled through Strong Eagle's mind. Jacqo would stay with Morning Dove, and she wouldn't leave her sisters. Aponi was attached to Andre. If he left, the loss would hurt. Would Andre's bond with her be enough to convince him to stay? We are more vulnerable without him. It's time to step in, into my father's place. Today I will call together a plan.

Andre and Strong Eagle spent the morning scouting their planned trail. It was wide enough for Willie to pull the travois, but they wouldn't know until they went further if they could get everything across the mountains. They walked back into camp at midday, greeting Aponi as she led Willie from the creek. Stopping by the chokecherry bushes, she reached up and pulled down a bunch, offering a berry to Etu, then another to Willie before tasting them herself, wrinkling her face at the sour taste.

At the fire awaited a feast. Morning Dove laid fresh greens and red raspberries around the steaming trout on a flat stone. She looked up and smiled as Jacqo returned with a tin of honey he found in his pack. He stirred it into the kettle of hot water filled with pine and juniper, stomach grumbling in anticipation. Strong Eagle looked up to see Raven standing on the rocks, Little Wolf at her side. She climbed down the stones, laughing at Little Wolf as he scrambled after her, nose quivering at the smells coming from the fire. Andre helped Aponi tie Willie to a tree near a patch of tall grass, and then they joined the group settling around the fire.

Strong Eagle held a gourd full of tea to the sky, to the earth, and then turning to each direction, he acknowledged all parts of the Sacred Circle. "I stand in gratitude for all that is before us." Taking courage from Raven's gentle presence, he let his eyes rest briefly on each person before speaking. "We'll feast together, then we must plan. It rained this morning, and soon snow will make the mountains impassable. We may travel for many days before finding a safe place." He smiled at Morning Dove and Aponi. "Raven wants to find your father's people. In times past, Lusio spoke of his homeland being across the mountains to the south. It'll be hard, but it will be worth it if we find his people." He looked around at the larger group, stopping at Andre. "You want to go east to find your and Jacqo's people. You say there is land to settle on where we would all be welcome." Jacqo looked uneasily from Strong Eagle to Andre, who remained silent.

"As we cross the mountains, we can decide what to do. We'll leave tomorrow."

Strong Eagle held out his hand to Raven, and together they carried the platter of food around the circle. Everyone's plate full, with little conversation, the group sat and ate. Little Wolf stayed at the edge, catching bits of food tossed to him.

Drifting apart, each began preparations for the journey. The sisters scrambled up and down the rocks as they brought everything down from the cave. Strong Eagle and Jacqo walked the path south again, clearing brush that might impede the travois. Andre set away from the group, occasionally looking up as he cleaned his musket.

"Where's Aponi?" Raven stepped down from the cave's rocks, alarm on her face. "And Willie?"

Andre felt his stomach sink. "You check around camp, and I'll check the river." Pushing brush out of the way, he followed the sounds of Willie's snorts, tied up near the river, grazing on sweetgrass. "Aponi?" He followed her footprints along the water's edge. "Aponi?"

Movement in the brush caught his attention. Stepping around, he found Aponi sitting on the ground with Little Wolf at her side. Hands held out, rainbow strands of light swirled from her palms, reaching for the sun. Little Wolf followed the light beams with his nose as they drifted upward. Butterflies glided in circles, weaving in and out of the strings of light. Andre stood in awe of her magic. Turning to footsteps behind him, he held his finger up to his mouth and pointed as Morning Dove and Raven approached. Morning Dove whispered in Raven's ear, who, with a look of alarm, put her hand over the secret pocket holding her talisman.

Raven looked up at Andre. "She's calling butterflies. Dada says her name means butterfly in his childhood tribe." A frown worked its way across her forehead. "To her, butterflies are friends, and it's natural to call them this way. But she doesn't know her power, and another tribe might accuse her of being a witch."

"She was doing this just before she fell in the river."

Aponi whispered in Etu's ear, then pointed at the butterflies. Giggling, one could almost hear Etu's giggle as well.

Morning Dove went to Aponi and squatted next to her, bringing her out of the trance. Startled, Aponi looked around at everyone with a sheepish look. "It's okay," Morning Dove whispered. "We were worried about you."

"I brought Little Wolf," Aponi said. "And Etu." She looked up at Raven and Andre, then past them as the butterflies spiraled into the sky. Morning Dove leaned over, a surprised look on her face as Aponi whispered in her ear.

Raven held her hand. "Come, Aponi, help us get packed. We're leaving on a journey in the morning."

Aponi stood, looking into the sky with longing, and then followed the group back to the camp. Morning Dove held Raven back and whispered. "She said Dada is coming."

Raven stood in silence. "It's what I pray for, but I'm afraid to hope."

Jacqo stood waiting at the tree line. "Everything all right?"

Andre nodded, leading Willie through the brush. "She's a special one, that girl."

Andre surveyed the packed travois as Raven and Strong Eagle brought the last skins and food cache from the cave late in the day. The skeleton of one teepee provided the base for the travois. They left the other intact in case they found the mountains unpassable and needed to return for shelter.

"We leave at first light." Strong Eagle said.

ELEVEN

The following day Lusio stood at the riverbank. Wading into the water, he looked down, startled as a catfish brushed his ankle. With perfect timing, he scooped the fish out of the water and tossed it onto the bank. Slipping in the mud as he climbed out, he fell on top of the fish, the razor-sharp barbs cutting his belly. Crying out in pain, he rolled off the fish, pulled out his knife, and chopped off its head.

Cleaned and gutted, he poked a sharp stick through it, then held it over a small fire, watching the juices sputter as it cooked. At the river, he flinched as he splashed cold water on the cuts, wishing for Aiyani's special salve and gentle touch as she smoothed it on his scrapes and scratches. Heavy with loss, he wondered if he would ever feel joy again. Sighing, with a full belly, he lay under the tree and slept. Lusio woke as the sun shifted behind the horizon to the west, and he prepared to continue his trek south in the dark of night.

Raven stood, looking at the empty cave and the drawings on the wall she made the day the sun died. She hoped her offering would appease the spirits and protect her daughter from harm. Little Wolf nuzzled her hand. Squatting down, she put her arm around his neck, feeling his coarse fur, reminded of the morning she first woke to find him nestled by her hip.

"Will you stay with us, or is your family waiting for you?" As glimmers of sun peeked through the fog, Raven climbed down the rocks, the pup close behind. She stood back for a moment, filled with gratitude as she watched the others. Andre secured the harness on Willie as Jacqo tied it to the travois. Strong Eagle came from the creek, bow and arrows slung across his back, carrying full water skins. He met her gaze and smiled.

"Let's go." Andre lifted Aponi onto Willie's back, Etu snugged in the bag hanging over her shoulder. Discretely the men had arranged the travois to accommodate Raven if she could not walk long distances. Strong Eagle had seen her holding her back, trying not to show pain, but he could see it in her eyes, and was worried. Now, insisting she was okay, she took her place next to him. He looked back at Andre, standing next to Willie. Exchanging nods, they set off, Jacqo and Morning Dove bringing up the rear.

Raven looked at the yucca bushes as they passed, one of the first things she discovered when contemplating the journey south to find her father's people. And now it was happening. She touched the talisman through the cloth of her dress, grateful for her mother's wisdom.

Everyone was quiet as they ascended the mountain. Sounds of the river grew distant as the trees thinned. Raven traded places with Andre, taking Willie's lead and walking with Aponi so the men could clear the brush blocking the trail. They found a grassy clearing to camp for the night. Jacqo secured Willie, then he and Andre set their bedrolls along the trees backing the woods. Morning Dove and Aponi lay their furs near the fire, while Strong Eagle and Raven lay theirs in the small clearing on the other side. Little Wolf was restless, pacing between Aponi and Raven, and soon wandered into the trees. Raven heard a pack of wolves howling in the distance. Would he be there come morning?

Thick, early morning fog greeted Lusio as he walked around the bend. Standing in a large grassy area, he could barely make out what looked like a fork in the trail ahead. He sensed he was getting closer but exhausted, dropped his pack on the ground and pulled out the last of the dried meat and berries. Hand halfway to his mouth, he stopped, sniffing the air. The scent of death was here. Uneasy, he unrolled his fur and lay down but couldn't sleep. Up again, Lusio unwrapped the leather from his ankle and brushed off the caked mud. Without the leather binding, his foot dropped limply to the side. Laying on his fur, he touched his knife before falling into a restless sleep. He dreamt of the chickadee, lavender, and Aiyani. Mid-dream, he woke with a start, squinting into the bright morning sunlight. Something was moving through the brush near the fork in the trail. Knife out, he stood and edged behind a tree. A young gray wolf, ears perked, poked his head out of the tall grass and looked straight into Lusio's eyes. For a moment, Lusio swore he was looking into the eyes of Lone Elk. Then, as quickly as he appeared, the wolf turned and disappeared behind the brush.

Lusio searched the area, finding the remains of the puma and more tracks. He looked up as the chickadee landed on the branch of a nearby mesquite bush. The dream of Aiyani still potent in his mind, he hastily rolled up the sleeping fur, stuffed the ankle leather in his pack, and pulled on his moccasins. The chickadee lifted off the branch, wings fluttering, and just as she'd done before, circled him three times and flew towards the fork in the trail. The same direction the young wolf had gone. Slowed by his injured ankle, he followed as fast as he could.

As the sun reached the midpoint of the sky, Lusio stepped into Raven's camp. A lone teepee stood at the edge of the woods. He looked up at the empty cave, then went over and felt the fire pit. *Still warm.*

Tentatively, Lusio walked to the teepee and untied the door, lifting it. It was empty except for a small pile of items wrapped in a soft rabbit fur blanket. He passed the fire pit in the center, noted fresh ash, and then knelt, running his hands over the soft fur blanket. Inside, he found dried meat and berries. A full skin of water leaned up against the back of the teepee. Someone left these things. *But who?*

Stepping out of the teepee, he looked over and saw the young gray wolf sitting near the trail. The pup stood, stared him in the eyes, then turned and trotted up the mountain, out of sight. The chickadee sat high in the pine, watching.

Hastily, Lusio pulled the leather strap out of his pack, wrapped his ankle, and pulled on his moccasins. Sleep forgotten, he folded the blanket inside his bedroll, shoved a piece of jerky into his mouth, and followed the trail in the direction of the wolf pup, passing the yucca plants as he began the ascent up the mountain.

Ignoring the pain in his foot, he walked until the blue sky turned violet and finally crimson. Ahead he could smell a campfire. Edging closer, he set his pack between two trees and raised his hands to his mouth. He made the call of a dove, drawing out the sound with the flicker of his fingers, repeating the call three times.

Strong Eagle walked the perimeter of their camp. He smiled at Morning Dove and Aponi asleep in their furs, then nodded to Andre as he led Willie back from a nearby creek. Jacqo lay in his bedroll, hat over his face. Satisfied, Strong Eagle walked towards the furs Raven laid out on the other side of the fire for them. The sound of a dove stopped him in his tracks. He looked over at Andre, musket already drawn. Jacqo, whom he knew hadn't been asleep, stood, pulling out his knife. Raven met him at the fire, worry on her face. He held his fingers up to his lips and pointed at her sisters. She went and sat next to them.

The brothers silently circled in opposite directions, Jacqo behind the sisters and Andre along the trees toward the trail leading back down the mountain. Strong Eagle pulled his knife out and edged his way past their sleeping furs. He answered the dove's call with the soft, hooting sounds of an owl three times, then moved down the trail a few steps.

"What's wrong?" Morning Dove whispered, rubbing eyes heavy with sleep.

"There is someone out there," Raven whispered back. "Shoosh," she whispered. Aponi stirred and opened her eyes. The three girls huddled together, watching.

Andre raised the musket as a man stepped out of the shadows and walked towards Strong Eagle, dragging his left foot.

"Háishą' ánít'į̇!" Strong Eagle called out.

"Lusio," the man answered.

"T'aa, aanii?" Strong Eagle asked, trying to look past Lusio and into the trees for others.

"Aoo," Lusio responded, walking towards Strong Eagle, hands held out, showing he was alone.

Andre stood with musket in hand, aimed at the trail, while Jacqo stood with the sisters.

Strong Eagle walked the short distance to Lusio. "It's you."

"Yes." He looked into Strong Eagle's eyes, then swooned into a faint.

Strong Eagle caught him in a hug. "Come."

The girls looked up as Strong Eagle led Lusio into the camp, his face's sharp angular bones reflected in the fire's light. "Dada?" Morning Dove whispered.

Lusio stared at them blankly, then looked at Strong Eagle. "Are they real?"

"Yes," Strong Eagle said. "Go." He held his arm around him as they circled the fire. Lusio knelt on the dirt before his daughters. Reaching out, he brushed Aponi's hair out of her eyes, hands trembling at the softness.

Aponi grinned. "I knew you would come, Dada. Etu told me, and the butterflies."

"Butterflies?" He mumbled, turning to Morning Dove and Raven. He touched their faces, still unsure if they were real. Morning Dove and Raven sat entranced, staring at their father.

"Mama? Chitto?" Lusio asked.

Raven shook her head sadly, eyes filling with tears.

"I'm sorry," Lusio faltered, unable to find words. "I wasn't there...."

Aponi scooted over and climbed onto his lap, leaning her head into his shoulder as she wrapped her arms around his neck. Lusio tensed at the touch, a touch he hadn't expected ever to feel again. She began to move away, but he held her tight. "No, stay."

Holding Aponi with one arm, he reached out to his daughters with the other.

The brothers stood back, watching for a moment, then busied themselves with tasks. Andre checked on Willie, and Jacqo rearranged his bedroll as Strong Eagle walked the camp's perimeter. Returning with Lusio's pack, he dropped it nearby. Lusio nodded thanks, leaned over, and lay Aponi, asleep, on her fur.

Lusio felt as if he were in a dream. Words came slowly. He looked up at Raven, standing next to Strong Eagle, her long hair shimmering against the light of the fire, noting the roundness of her belly against her dress. She smiled and walked toward him, handing him a plate of food.

"You are a woman now," Lusio said. "Mama would be proud." He brushed her hair with his fingers.

"Strong Eagle and I married. I am with child." She smiled, holding her hand over her round belly. "I wanted to go south, to look for your family, and you."

"I can take you there." He looked around the group, resting his eyes on Jacqo and Andre.

Morning Dove nestled into Lusio's shoulder. "Strong Eagle said you would find us."

"I am grateful. Someone left my things in our teepee."

Morning Dove smiled. "I knew you would come back." She leaned over and kissed her father on the cheek. "Good night, Dada. I'm happy you are here." She crawled into her fur next to Aponi.

Lusio looked up as Strong Eagle walked over, squatting next to them. Reaching out, he put his hand on Raven's shoulder, then caressed her cheek. "You need to sleep."

She looked up at him, then turned back to Lusio, covering his hands with hers. "Will you sleep?"

"I have my pack," Lusio said. "And someone left food wrapped in a rabbit blanket."

"Ah...." Raven stood. "I collected rabbit skins and made the blanket. I hope it keeps you warm." Lusio looked into his daughter's eyes, seeing the warmth and wisdom of Aiyani, his heart torn between gratitude and loss. "I love you, Dada." The men watched her walk to the fur she laid out earlier.

Strong Eagle looked up as Andre nodded good night, then sat next to Lusio by the fire. He told him about the massacre and events that followed. Lusio shared his story and told him of finding his boyhood village by the Zuni River. "I will take us there. Lolotea and Hotda will help Raven give birth to your child."

"Ahéhee," Strong Eagle held his hands over his heart in thanks. " We hoped to get across the mountains before the snow came," Strong Eagle said. "We can stay here part of the day tomorrow, but we should keep moving." Lusio nodded in agreement. "Will it take a long time to reach your village?"

Lusio looked up as a star streaked across the night sky. "If we can cross the mountains before heavy snows, one or two moons. We will be there in time for Shalako."

"Shalako?"

"For the Zuni, it's the biggest celebration of the year. On the darkest night, we dance, welcoming back the light."

Strong Eagle glanced at Lusio, uncertainty flashing in his eyes. "Will we be accepted there?"

"Yes. You'll see."

Strong Eagle joined Raven, and soon all were asleep except for Lusio, who sat gazing into the shapes that drifted in and out of the flames, tossing in wood to keep the fire burning bright against the cold mountain air, the soft rabbit fur blanket wrapped around him.

Hours later, a gentle shaking of his shoulder woke him. Morning Dove stood, the morning sun shining through the trees, reflecting on her hair. She held out a gourd of hot tea. His hand shook as he reached for it. Sitting next to him, she steadied his hand as she put the cup in it, then leaned into his shoulder. They looked up as Raven and Aponi came out of the trees and into the camp, with Little Wolf following behind. Aponi giggled as Little Wolf nuzzled her hand. She reached into her dress pocket and pulled out a piece of jerky, letting him lick it out of her palm. Raven looked across the fire at her father and smiled at the shocked look on his face.

"Little Wolf came to me soon after I found the cave." Raven joined them and told the story.

"He led me here," Lusio said. "I'm grateful, but I have never seen a wolf act like this."

"Nothing is like it used to be." Raven smiled at Aponi and Little Wolf. "I wonder if he will stay with us. I heard a pack of wolves howling last night."

Lusio sat quietly by the fire, then looked up at Raven. Seeing his grief-stricken eyes, she sat beside him and lay her head on his shoulder. "Mama was running, trying to warn me. I saw her fall. I got away and came back the next morning. Chitto lay dead next to the tree. I thought everyone was dead. Then I heard men's voices moving towards me. I was scared. I ran. I'm sorry, Dada."

Lusio reached over and took her hand. "Mama lives in your eyes."

Raven held his gaze, reaching out to touch him. "I miss her. And Chitto."

Morning Dove covered their hands with hers. "When I have a child, I will name him Chitto."

Aponi knelt in front of them, holding out her doll. "Etu." She pulled the arrow out of her bag. "Chitto's arrow. Raven said he is our Spirit Warrior now. He will protect us."

Lusio sat frozen as mixed waves of joy and grief washed over him. Reaching out, he touched the arrow, then the doll, stroking the long, purple cornsilk braid. "She's... she's beautiful." He looked up as Andre walked by. The two men's eyes met, then Andre looked away, turning his back to the group.

Aponi put her ear to Etu and then pointed up at a nearby pine. "Mama."

The group looked up at the yellow-bellied chickadee as she sat on a branch, her wings sparkling in the sunlight as they fluttered.

"Mama?" Lusio asked. "The chickadee was with me in the old village, then I saw it along the trail." The truth registered on his face. "She was with me every day." He flashed on the first time he saw the wolf pup and seeing Lone Elk in his eyes. "Little Wolf and chickadee led me here... Aiyani... Lone Elk..."

"When I woke after the massacre, the chickadee was there," Strong Eagle said. "We've all seen it."

"I dreamt of her when I was in the moon lodge." Morning Dove said.

"Of the Chickadee?' Or Mama?" Lusio paused, then looked up at her. "Moon Lodge?"

"Yes, I am a woman now." She blushed. "I dreamt of both. Mama told me to follow the chickadee."

Strong Eagle lay a flat rock over the fire and placed the fish on top. Soon the juices dripped down, making the fire sputter as the scent of fish cooking filled the air. The chickadee flew off the branch, circled the group three times, then flew away into the trees.

"Her job is done." Strong Eagle said as the chickadee flew away. "Her Spirit can rest now."

Lusio stood as if to follow, wanting only to be with Aiyani. He looked at his daughters and torn, impulsively took a step toward the woods. His ankle gave out and he fell to the ground.

"Dada!" Morning Dove rushed to him as Jacqo and Strong Eagle helped him up.

"When the soldiers captured me, they tied a rope around my ankle to keep me from running away." Lusio spat on the ground. "Ruined me."

"Here, lie on your fur." Raven helped him lay down as Morning Dove pulled off his moccasin and removed the leather wrap. Strong Eagle squatted down and looked at it.

"It will take time." Morning Dove watched as he moved the foot in a circle, feeling the bones in the ankle and foot. "It is not broken." She wrapped the leather around it snuggly and put his moccasin back on. "Does this help?"

Lusio nodded. Overwhelmed, he wanted to run, escape from the turmoil racing through him, but pain held him in the moment. He looked up, searching the tree for the chickadee.

"Rest, Dada." Morning Dove tucked the rabbit fur blanket around him.

"We need to keep moving," Lusio said. "Get across the mountains."

"Rest while we get ready." Morning Dove looked down at her father as he closed his eyes and then at her sisters. Raven offered her hand, and the sisters stood, arms around each other, gazing up into the tree where the chickadee had sat only a moment ago.

The group left as the sun reached the midpoint in the sky. Andre joined Strong Eagle and Raven in the front while Lusio walked next to Aponi, astride Willie. Andre looked over his shoulder, meeting Lusio's eyes in a hard stare before looking away.

Lusio had seen the hurt on Andre's face when Aponi crawled onto his lap and hugged him. And he knew Andre had given her the doll. Everything was happening so fast. He didn't know his place in this new family.

Almost to the top, they found a clearing near a small creek to camp for the night. Lusio built a fire and sat stoking it, looking up as Strong Eagle returned with trout dangling from a string. Together they prepared the fish. Laying the flattest stone they could find over the fire, the smell soon permeated the air, drawing the group together where they sat silently and ate. Hunger satisfied, soon all lay wrapped in their bedrolls asleep.

Lusio lay under the rabbit fur blanket. He dreamt of Chitto, his laughter filling his heart, just as it had in life. In the dream, Chitto held out closed fists. "Choose a hand, Dada." Lusio tapped his left hand. Chitto opened it. It was empty. The dream shifted to his grandfather, lying before him on his deathbed. "Honor your medicine... choose wisely." Then Lusio dreamt of the chickadee. The bird faded as Aiyani came into view, carrying branches of lavender. She looked at him and blew him a kiss. And then she was gone.

The group continued the trek up the mountain at sunrise the next day. As the sun moved west on the horizon and they neared the top, Willie snorted in protest at the weight he pulled behind him.

Limping, Lusio took Raven's arm and joined Strong Eagle on an outcrop of rocks, looking out at the vista below and the next mountain they would cross. Lusio pointed to smaller peaks in the far distance. "The Big River on the other side of these mountains, we will follow it to the Zuni River and my childhood home."

"How long?" Strong Eagle asked.

"Once we get across these mountains, if we make it before snow, about ten sunrises." Lusio shaded his eyes with his hand as a hawk glided into view, circling down from a crest of rocks above them. Golden waves of feathers shimmered in the afternoon sun, its sharp, black talons taut in long slender legs. In an instant, the hawk drew up its body, then plummeted toward the rock ledge, pouncing on its target with wings and nose down. Raven shuddered, a chill running down her spine. She reached down, touching the talisman, then looked up as the hawk lifted a snake, writhing in the powerful grip of the large bird.

"Something is coming," Lusio said. "We must be ready."

TWELVE

Raven clenched her hand around the talisman. The memory of her mother came to her, offering comfort yet leaving her confused as she held the small stone.

"Trust this," Aiyani had said, handing the stone to her young daughter as she held her hand over her heart. "Trust yourself. You will always know what to do." As her fingers rolled across the stone, worn smooth over time, she knew her mother would always be with her. All she needed to do was listen.

Strong Eagle stood, arm around Raven, watching as the hawk flew upwards, a snake now hanging limp from its talons. As it landed on the crest of rocks above, they could see strands of grass hanging out of a crevice.

"She hunts to feed her young." Lusio shuddered, shaking a sense of unease off his shoulders.

Strong Eagle and Lusio exchanged a look as they turned to go back to the camp. Lusio tripped on a fallen branch, wincing in pain. Strong Eagle caught him. "We'll make room for you on the travois." Lusio nodded, head hung in frustration.

"It'll take time, Dada." Raven took Lusio's arm, supporting him.

"Yes. But..."

Raven squeezed his arm as they approached the group.

"This is a good place to stop and rest," Andre said, watching as Morning Dove lay a fur on the ground for her father. And without hesitation, the group stepped into their new routine. Soon, Jacqo had a fire blazing, Willie grazed, and food was gathered and set out around the fire. Then, as darkness filled the sky and the world around them became still, they sat together, eating in silence. One by one, bellies full, they drifted to their sleeping furs and bedrolls.

The morning chatter of birds filled the air as the new daylight filtered through the high mountain pines. Lusio lay with his eyes closed, breathing the warm and woodsy scent of the trees. There had only been patches of snow in the shade, but today felt different. The air was crisper, colder. He listened for the chickadee's familiar song, but the birds' chatter no longer held Aiyani's presence. It was time for him to wake and lead the remaining survivors to his childhood village. Opening his eyes, he looked over as Jacqo stirred the fire and Morning Dove made tea. *They are good together. Natural.*

He smiled, remembering his courtship with Aiyani so many years ago. *I miss you, Aiyani, my wife. I will take care of our daughters.*

"Good morning, Dada." He hadn't heard Aponi's approach. He smiled at her, hair braided and Etu tucked in the bag under her arm. Reaching up, he pulled her down and into a hug, tickling her. The air sparkled with her laughter. Holding her a moment longer, Aponi squirmed out of the hug, running over to Willie. Jacqo secured the lead on the mule and smiled down at her, now whispering a secret in Willie's ear.

"Ready?" Strong Eagle asked, reaching down to offer Lusio a hand. "We made room for you on the travois." Lusio frowned. "It'll be easier for you to walk once we get to the top."

Settled on the travois, Lusio and Strong Eagle looked down at Aponi, who stared at the trail behind them. Little Wolf was standing at the edge of the trees. Aponi took a step towards him, reaching her hand into her pocket, her bag with Etu falling on the ground.

Strong Eagle caught her arm, pointing. "No, look." Behind Little Wolf was a large, dark gray wolf. The two wolves watched for a moment, then turned and trotted away down the mountain trail.

Raven knelt and put her arm around Aponi. "He has found his family," she said. "I heard them howling last night. They were calling him."

"It's best," Strong Eagle said. Lusio nodded in agreement. Aponi stared at the space the wolves occupied a moment ago, then climbed up onto the travois with Lusio, tucking her head into his shoulder. For the first time since the massacre, she cried.

"You have Willie, my little one." Lusio hugged her as she sobbed into his shoulder. "And when we get to the village, there are dogs. Horses too."

"Dogs? Horses?" Aponi looked up, cheeks smudged with glistening tears.

"Yes, horses are like Willie." He smiled, pulling her closer. "But bigger. You'll see."

Aponi lay her head on his chest.

Andre stood by Willie with his back to the group, listening. At Aponi's sobs, he turned. Lusio looked up, meeting Andre's stare. He saw the tension in his jaw and pain in his eyes. In the past, he had seen the way Andre looked at Aiyani. *What happened? Surely Aiyani wouldn't. But I wasn't there.*

Andre walked over and picked up Aponi's bag from the ground, holding Etu. He tucked it into her arms, then looked hard at Lusio before turning and walking into the trees.

A moment later, Morning Dove and Jacqo came out of the bushes laughing, arms full of fresh roots and berries. Raven and Strong Eagle looked up, a smile passing between them.

Andre watched, hidden in the shadows of the trees. *They're happy, Jacqo's content, but is there a place for me?* His shoulders hung as he felt the disappointment of his hopes and dreams pushed to the side.

Steps slowed, and the group lagged as they neared the top of the mountain. Jacqo looked at Andre in alarm at the sound of someone chopping wood. "Wait here," he said, catching Strong Eagle's eye.

THIRTEEN

Strong Eagle motioned for Morning Dove and Raven to join him next to the travois. Holding his finger up to the sisters, he laid his hand on Willie, who snorted displeasure at the disruption.

Andre pulled his musket out and nodded to Jacqo. Together they went ahead, staying out of sight at the edge of the trees. As they neared the clearing, they saw the figure of a large man with bushy brown hair, holding an ax high over his head. He swung the ax down, neatly splitting a log in half. Nearby lay a stack of skins, pelts, and furs. The big man lifted the ax over his head again, then stopped, sensing their presence.

The brothers glanced at each other. Andre lowered his musket to the ground, but Jacqo kept his hand on the knife in his belt. "Mountain Mike," Andre said.

"Andre, Jacqo?" Mountain Mike studied the men, giving them a curt nod. He set the ax head on the ground, leaning slightly on it. "What brings you to these parts?"

"We're leading a party across the mountain," Andre said. He briefly told him about the massacre. "They're headed south to the Zuni River, getting over the mountains before the snow. They mean no harm."

"Humph." Mountain Mike scratched his crotch and raised eyebrows as bushy as the hair on his head. "Well, where are they?"

Andre whistled. Raven and Strong Eagle stepped into the clearing, leading the rest. Aponi sat on the travois as Lusio and Morning Dove walked behind.

"This is Mountain Mike," Jacqo started. "Our paths have crossed in the fur trading business."

Andre tightened his grip on the musket as the big man sized up the group. Jacqo stepped back towards the travois, a glance passing between him and Strong Eagle.

Mountain Mike looked at the sisters, at the mule, then the loaded travois. His scowl turned into a broad grin and he held his arms out in welcome. "Come on now. Rest by the fire."

Andre nodded to Jacqo, who pulled Willie and the travois past Mountain Mike. He unhooked the mule and led him into the trees towards the sound of running water. Aponi whispered in Raven's ear, who motioned to Morning Dove. The sisters stepped into the woods. While Strong Eagle waited for them, Lusio approached the men at the campfire. Mountain Mike watched, a curious look in his eyes.

"Injured?" Mountain Mike asked, noting Lusio's limp.

"Soldiers," Andre said.

Mountain Mike nodded. "They've been raising hell around these parts. Some of 'em got a little crazy."

"Ones who attacked the village are dead." Andre took a drink out of a waterskin, then spat on the ground. "Mean bastards."

"Good." Mountain Mike said, looking up as the sisters emerged from the woods with Strong Eagle and Jacqo, leading Willie close behind.

"There's a stream on the other side of the trees," Jacqo said, tying Willie to a branch.

Mountain Mike nodded. "Got me a deer over there last night." He nodded at the makeshift rack he made over the fire to smoke the meat. "She was drinking out of the creek. Easy kill." He went over and took a piece of meat, dropping it on a flat stone over the fire.

Morning Dove walked over to the travois, pulled a skin off, and brought it over to him. She opened it and laid out the roots, greens and berries they had gathered earlier in the day. Mountain Mike nodded in appreciation, then walked over to the woodpile, returning with an armful and dropping it on the ground.

"There's a good place to camp near the stream," Jacqo said to Strong Eagle. "Andre and I will stay with Willie and the travois." Strong Eagle nodded.

"We'll be on our way at first light." Andre looked pointedly at Mountain Mike as he put his musket in the sling over his shoulder. Mountain Mike squatted by the fire, digging his fingers into his beard, scratching his chin. He looked across the fire at Aponi, berries in hand, big eyes watching him. She leaned over, whispered in Etu's ear, then scooted closer to Lusio. Chuckling, Mountain Mike pulled out a flask and offered it to Andre.

Andre held up his hand. "No, thank ya. I know your whiskey." He smiled, shaking his head.

Mountain Mike grinned. "Nice mule you have there."

"Ah, Willie," Jacqo said, squatting next to the fire. "We traded for him a couple of villages back." Mountain Mike offered him the flask. "Nah, thanks anyway."

"My mule went lame... had to shoot 'em. Pitiful thing." Mountain Mike glanced up at Andre. "Would sure be nice to have another. You're planning on going to the Zuni with them?" He shook his head and spat. "Spanish soldiers everywhere down there. Coming up from the south."

Andre looked up at Jacqo. "I was hoping to head east. Heard rumors Huguenots were settling out east in Virginia Territory. Rumors are there's free land. Feel ready to settle down."

"I was ready to pack up and head that way myself." Mountain Mike nodded to the stack of skins and pelts nearby. "Happy to have some company." Andre nodded but remained silent, looking up at the light shining through the trees as the sun fell to the west.

"Chow," Mountain Mike called out. As the group gathered around the fire, he let his eyes rest on each person, taking another sip out of his flask. "Keeps a man warm on a cold mountain night," he chuckled, catching Morning Dove's eye.

Lusio put his arm around his daughter. The group sat quietly and ate as Willie snorted, eating grass nearby. Mountain Mike sipped on his whisky, his gaze wandering to the mule and the travois, then back to Morning Dove.

"Time to rest." Strong Eagle stood, lifting Aponi into his arms. He led Raven to their camp near the creek, where he had built a small fire. Lusio and Morning Dove followed. Mountain Mike stood behind the fire, watching from the corner of his eye as they disappeared into the trees.

"Sure you don't want a nip to ward off the chill?" Mountain Mike held out the flask to Jacqo.

"Nah." Jacqo held up his hand in protest. "Morning will come early enough."

"Any chance they might change their mind and come east?" Mountain Mike asked, nodding to the group retreating into the trees. "It's gonna be hard getting a travois across those mountains."

Jacqo shrugged and looked away.

"They're set on finding Lusio's people," Andre said. "Better for Raven and the baby."

"Think on it," Mountain Mike said. "If you want to come east, I know the settlement you're talking about. Near the trading post."

Andre stood and nodded. "Night." He and Jacqo went over to their bedrolls near the travois.

"Would you come?" Andre asked in the dark, wrapping his blanket around him.

Jacqo was quiet for a moment. "I've spent every day of my life with you. I can't imagine otherwise. But I want to stay with them. I want to marry Morning Dove."

"She could come with us," Andre countered. "We could all start fresh."

"She won't leave her sisters, and they want to go to Lusio's people," Jacqo said. "Won't you come? At least check it out?"

Andre didn't respond. He lay in the dark, awake, listening as Mountain Mike moved about the camp. He had seen the way he eyed the sisters. And the travois. Dealings in the past taught him Mountain Mike was a loner, and whiskey made him unpredictable. It would be best to separate the group from him as soon as possible.

"I'll take the first watch," Andre said. "Tired. Better if I sit up."

Jacqo lay in his bedroll, anxious thoughts preventing sleep. He heard Andre get up and walk past the travois down the trail. Mountain Mike had been restless, wandering around the camp, and soon, his footsteps followed Andres. Was he waiting for them to go to sleep? Jacqo got up and followed. It surprised him to see Andre talking to Mountain Mike. He edged closer.

"The travois?" Mountain Mike asked.

"Don't think so." Andre looked over his shoulder.

"And what about the girl?"

"No, not the girl," Andre said.

Mountain Mike persisted. "I want the travois. And the girl."

The men looked over as Jacqo edged behind a tree, kicking a stone loose. The men froze, looking around. Afraid they'd seen him, Jacqo snuck back to his bedroll. What was his brother thinking? Mountain Mike was bad news.

Andre looked Mountain Mike in the eye. "We'll leave at first light. All of us, with the travois and the mule. You can forget you ever saw us."

Mountain Mike watched Andre walk away, eyes narrowed and hard.

Jacqo heard Andre's approach and feigned sleep as his brother stood looking down at him and then, after hearing him settle, drifted into an uneasy sleep. Neither heard Mountain Mike creep into the woods.

Morning Dove woke with an urgent need to pee. She heard the soft sounds of Aponi's breathing and looked over at Lusio, rolled up in his blanket. Raven and Strong Eagle were asleep across the fire. Quietly, she stole out of her fur and went behind the nearest tree.

Lusio heard his daughter get up and followed. Mountain Mike made him uneasy, and he didn't like how the big man looked at Morning Dove. He was eager to get the group to the safety of his village. Sensing motion in the trees, he pulled out his knife. A rabbit darted out of the grass as Morning Dove returned. Relieved, he shadowed her as she walked back, and they crawled back into their bedrolls, unaware Mountain Mike stood in the trees, watching.

Mountain Mike stumbled back to the fire and fell into his bedroll.

What is he up to? Andre wondered. Soon, loud snoring from Mountain Mike's bedroll assured Andre it was safe to sleep for a little while.

Sounds of movement in the camp woke Mountain Mike. He sat up, scratching his head, squinting into the morning light. He looked over as Strong Eagle lifted Aponi onto the travois.

Andre came over. "Heading out."

Mountain Mike stood and shook his hand. He noticed a bundle near the fire. "Forget sumthin?"

"They left a bundle of roots and berries for you. It's their way." Andre said.

Mountain Mike looked over and waved to the group. "I'll be packin' up today and heading out myself. I'll catch up with y'all later."

Andre nodded. "We're headed down the mountain. Should be down by nightfall."

"What we talked about... think on it." Mountain Mike said.

Andre scowled at him. "You mean what you talked about."

Mountain Mike watched as they left, travois dragging on the ground behind the mule, then turned, tossing his meager belongings together. Rifle, tomahawk and his possibles bag, flint, extra knife, sharp bones, and the last of sinew for mending clothes. The travois would have been nice. And the girl. It'd been a while since he had a woman. Too long. Picking up a flask nearby, he drained it, caught the last few drops of whiskey, then tossed it onto the pile. Tying his frayed rope together, he wound it around the stack of pelts and furs in a tight bundle, leaving enough to make a sling so he could carry it on his back. He could catch the group by midday if he hurried. He had some thinkin' to do. He wanted the travois. And the girl.

FOURTEEN

Just past midday and hot, Andre wiped the sweat from his forehead with his sleeve. Strong Eagle raised his hand for the group to stop, pointing to a sharp bend in the trail ahead of them.

"Not sure the travois will make it." Jacqo peered down the sharp drop-off as he edged around the travois.

His moccasins slipped in the dry, loose dirt. Toes clenched, he dug them into the dirt through the soft leather. Bracing himself, he shoved the travois sideways.

Aponi jumped off the travois as Andre unhooked Willie, tossing the rein to Raven. Andre lifted the front of the travois. "Push from behind, and I'll try to angle the travois from here."

"Right." Jacqo grabbed a pack as it fell off the travois and tossed it to Lusio. Turning back around, his foot slipped.

Morning Dove screamed as Jacqo fell, his hat twirling in the air. Jacqo grabbed the base of the travois with one hand, feet dangling into the ravine, his weight pulling the travois closer to the edge.

"Jacqo!" Andre yelled, dropping the travois. He ran to the side, using his weight to stop it from going over. Strong

Eagle grabbed on, helping to pull the travois away from the edge. Lusio joined Andre, but his foot gave out, and he rolled to the ground.

"Hold it," Strong Eagle said to Andre.

"Got it."

Strong Eagle jumped across the travois, holding his hand down to Jacqo. Their fingers brushed. Using his feet to anchor himself in the packs on the travois, Strong Eagle hoisted himself forward.

Raven gasped, hand clutched around the puma tooth. Aponi buried her face in Willie's neck.

Jacqo looked up, blinking as sweat rolled into his eyes. "Ahggg..." His shoulder burned, but he stretched his fingers a little further. Just as his other hand, slick with sweat, slipped off the travois, Strong Eagle grabbed his arm. Using his feet and legs to pull himself backward, Strong Eagle pulled Jacqo up and over the travois. The two men fell in a heap next to Lusio. Stunned, the group watched as the travois slipped over the edge, falling apart as it tumbled down into the ravine.

"My dress, my beads." The bundle with Raven's wedding dress pulled apart, the beads and feathers sparkling as they fluttered in the air.

"What will we do? Our food, pottery." Morning Dove cried as the sisters huddled together. "Everything from our village… my moon basket, Mama's herbs." They turned at the sound of Jacqo groaning, cradling his right arm.

Andre dropped to the ground and felt Jacqo's shoulder. "Shoulder's out. Lay down." He supported Jacqo as he rolled onto his back, sweat rolling off his face. Strong Eagle knelt on Jacqo's left side while Morning Dove sat with her head buried in Lusio's shoulder.

"Hold him," Andre said to Strong Eagle, pulling Jacqo's arm out.

Jacqo winced, gritting his teeth. "Just do it!"

Andre used his foot to press against Jacqo's side, tugging on his extended arm.

"Oh, dear Jesus," Jacqo's jaw clenched, then relaxed as his arm popped. "It's back in." He looked up at Andre, then turned ashen, rolled to the side, and retched.

Morning Dove came over and smoothed his hair off his face, holding it back as Jacqo emptied his stomach. She wiped his mouth and helped him to sit up. Jacqo wiped the sweat out of his eyes with his shirt sleeve and took the water she held out to him.

Lusio limped over, picked up the pack Jacqo had thrown to him, and opened it. His shoulders dropped in relief at the sight of dried meat and berries, lying on top of scraps of cloth, sinew, and bone needles. He pulled out the fabric and fashioned a sling.

"Here." Morning Dove held up Jacqo's arm as Lusio secured the sling.

"Gonna be hard to travel this way," Jacqo protested.

"Hurt less." Lusio stood and limped back to the remaining pack, examining the bits of jerky and berries. "There are caves along the way where we can sleep and streams where we can fish." He looked up at faces still in shock. "We'll get by. Everyone has their pack and a waterskin?"

Andre peered over the edge, then looked at the group. "I'm sorry." He turned and headed over to Willie. Picking up the loose lead lying on the ground, he handed it to Aponi and walked away.

Jacqo squeezed Morning Dove's hand and followed his brother. "It's not your fault."

"You could have died."

"But I didn't. You saved me, just as you always have."

"Strong Eagle saved you." Andre looked up. "I didn't."

"You and Strong Eagle." Jacqo winced in pain as he reached out to touch his brother's shoulder, surprised when Andre pulled away. "We're all family now. Please, don't do this."

Andre opened his pack and, with pained eyes, removed the Huguenot Cross. "Take this. I should have shared it with you a long time ago. It's our heritage."

"What are you saying?" Jacqo whispered. "Why now?"

"There's no place for me here." Andre could not keep the hurt out of his voice. "At the first opportunity, I'll leave and head out east. I want to find our people." Unhooking his waterskin from his belt, he drained the last out of it. "I hoped you would change your mind. Come with me."

Jacqo looked at his brother with grief-stricken eyes. "Huguenots may be our blood, but they haven't been our family for years." He looked over at the rest of the group. "This is our family now. Can't you see?"

"I have to go," Andre said. "Maybe I'll come back. But I must try. For Mother and Father." He kicked a pebble with his boot." I must see if there are any roots left that mean anything."

"Keep the cross." Jacqo put it in his brother's hand, closing Andre's fingers over it. "You may need it. It will prove who you are, and it may have value."

Andre opened his hand and turned the cross over, looking at the initials and date his mother etched on the back. "You might be right. I just thought after all this time. I should have..."

"It's all right." Jacqo reached down and touched the cross. "I saw it in your pack a while back."

Mountain Mike strode down the trail at a quick pace. When Morning Dove screamed, he dropped his things on the ground and jogged down, stopping behind a tall pine, watching as the travois tumbled into the ravine. Scowling, he spat on the ground as Morning Dove leaned into Jacqo, stroking his hair. Mountain Mike took a drink, feeling the heat of whisky hit the back of his throat.

Is the girl worth it? His loins answered for him. He gathered up his things and followed.

Dark clouds threatened rain as they followed the rough, winding trail to the bottom of the mountain. Except for the occasional skirmish of squirrels, silence prevailed.

Lusio kept on despite the pain in his ankle, his limp more pronounced with each step. "If we can get a little further, there is a safe place to sleep and water nearby." He looked around at tired faces. Strong Eagle picked up Aponi, who lay her head on his shoulder and closed her eyes as the group trudged on.

Morning Dove felt the urge to pee. She rubbed her back, easing the ache, which worsened with day's end. All the herbs from the old village had fallen into the ravine with the travois. Stopping at the side of the trail, she picked spiky, yellow flowers, then grabbed a sharp stick and dug up the roots. Brushing the dirt off, she bit off a piece. Bitterness filled her mouth, making her eyes water. Jacqo looked down in concern. She just shook her head and took a drink from her waterskin.

As purples turned to gray and a mist of rain fell around them, they came upon small niches under rock overhangs. Raven walked over to one, running her hand over the rough sandstone. Peeking in, she turned and looked at her father in surprise.

"The stones will keep us safe," Lusio said. "We'll stay here and sleep, but we need to keep going, can't risk getting stuck in the mountains."

Raven gathered the waterskins as Strong Eagle searched for his fishing line in the small bag hanging off his belt. He held it up, and together they disappeared into the trees, following the trickling sound of a nearby stream. Morning Dove gathered wood for a fire, stacking it in the crook of Jacqo's good arm before gathering up what she could carry. Stacking the wood, Jacqo watched as Andre ducked under the rock overhang, shooing a weasel out.

How could he think there's no place for him?

Strong Eagle and Raven returned with full waterskins and three large trout hanging off a string. Soon, the fish, cleaned and gutted, sputtered as it dripped into the fire, roasting on green willow sticks. Morning Dove opened the pack of berries as the group ate in silence.

Lusio stood and removed the rabbit skin blanket from his pack, laying it in a nearby cave. "You and Aponi can sleep here," he said to Morning Dove. "I'll be nearby." He nodded good night to Raven and Strong Eagle as they slipped into a small cave nearby.

"We'll stay by the fire." Andre shivered in the fall mountain night air. "Wonder where Mountain Mike ended up? Thought we would have seen him by now."

"Best if we don't," Jacqo said. "He's bad news."

"I'll take first watch." Andre sat on the ground with his back against a tree. But the strain of the day was too much, and soon he was fast asleep.

Mountain Mike stood in the trees and watched. He tilted the flask and let the last few drops of whiskey trickle down his throat.

Jacqo lay restless on the ground near the fire, the ache in his shoulder worse in the cold air. Yanking off the sling, he tossed it aside. *Should have packed more things on Willie. Everything was on the travois.* Raising his head, Jacqo looked up as Morning Dove stirred. He knew she wasn't feeling well and listened as she stole from the shelter, going behind the nearest tree. Lusio's shadow crossed the fire as he followed her.

Morning Dove squatted to pee, her insides burning as urine flowed out. Reaching into her pocket, she broke off a piece of the bitter root and put it in her mouth. She didn't hear the footsteps behind her.

Mountain Mike clamped his hand over her mouth, picked her up, and carried her under his arm. She kicked and struggled as his long stride took them through the trees and across the stream. The metallic taste of blood filled her mouth as she bit him.

"Gonna have to do better than that, girlie," he whispered, foul-smelling spittle spewing out of his mouth. "Don't think I've been bit before?" Grunting, he pulled the sweaty kerchief off his neck and tied it around her mouth. "There, that'll teach ya."

The smell of whiskey and sweat made her retch. Vomit filled her mouth.

Mountain Mike dropped her on the ground, unbuckling his pants.

Kicking as hard as she could, he cried out as her foot hit his crotch, and stumbled backward. Rolling away, she jumped up, frantically looking for a way out. Grabbing her dress, he spun her around, pushed her onto the ground, then kneeled, pinning her with his knee. In the struggle, he didn't hear Lusio come up behind him. Morning Dove looked up in terror at her father, who held his finger to his lips. The knife went in under the big man's rib cage, up and into Mountain Mike's heart, killing him instantly. The brothers came into the clearing just as Lusio pulled his knife out, the big man falling on top of Morning Dove.

"What the hell?" Jacqo said. The brothers ran over and rolled Mountain Mike off Morning Dove. Lusio helped her up and pulled the rancid cloth off her mouth. She knelt and vomited.

"Where did he come from?" Andre looked from Jacqo to Lusio and back to Jacqo.

"He must have grabbed her. I saw her go into the trees." Jacqo said. They stood back as Lusio walked her over to the stream. "I couldn't sleep, and I woke you when she didn't come back."

"Sneaky bastard." Andre's eyes were dark with rage. "Thank God for Lusio."

Easing her down into soft pine needles, Lusio took off his bandana, wetting it in the stream. Morning Dove leaned into him as he washed her face, then held her as she cupped water in her hands, rinsing out her mouth. "Did he hurt you?" Lusio asked as she sobbed in his arms.

"No... Yes..." she said. "I thought I would die there... like before." Morning Dove whispered, voice cracking.

"You're safe now." Lusio pulled her close. "I've got you," he repeated.

"Thank you, Dada." Morning Dove nestled into his shoulder. "I'm glad you are here."

124

She felt hot and feverish. Lusio looked over at the brothers, who rolled the big man into the nearby brush.

"Can't bury 'em," Jacqo said. "The shovel was on the travois."

"He had tools. Wonder where he stashed them?" Andre looked at his brother. "Careful of your arm."

Jacqo nodded dismissively. "Can't be far. We could use the tools."

Andre spat onto the ground. "The coyotes will take care of him."

Strong Eagle found Lusio and Morning Dove at the stream. "What happened?"

"Mountain Mike," Andre said. "He grabbed Morning Dove and tried to take her. Lusio killed him." He nodded in the direction they came from. "We drug him over there."

"Morning Dove is hot," Lusio tightened his arm around his daughter. "She's sick."

"I dug roots along the way. They will help." Reaching down, she gasped. "My pouch. It's gone."

Jacqo appeared, handing it to her. "Found this on the ground over there."

Relief flooded Morning Dove's face. Lusio looked up at Jacqo, then back at his daughter. With his good arm, Jacqo reached down and offered Morning Dove his hand. Lusio watched as the pair crossed the creek, pondering the bond forming between the two. A gringo. He wanted his daughter to be happy. Before, he would have questioned it. And now? He could still feel the touch of Aiyani's hand as they sat around the fire. Without her, a part of his soul was missing. But he could still imagine the touch. Would he deny the same to his daughter? Jacqo was tender with Morning Dove as he helped her over the tree roots so she wouldn't stumble. They were good together, and he wouldn't deny her this. The world was changing. Indeed, his had imploded. Suddenly, the urge to get them safely to the Zuni pueblo surged through him.

Raven paced by the fire, holding the talisman over her heart. Morning Dove needed her. Looking down at Aponi, snugged in the rabbit skin blanket next to Willie, asleep, she worried. Aponi whispered to Etu more than her sisters... her connection to Willie, the ability to call butterflies had always been amusing. But would the new tribe see it that way? The talisman grew warm in her hand. She reached into the warmth, seeking wisdom. The mule snickered, nuzzling his nose against Aponi's cheek. Would her connection to nature and animals be enough to protect her? Can we protect her from the world?

"Strong Eagle," Raven exclaimed as he came into view. "What happened?" As the rest of the group filtered into the camp, he stood by the fire, telling her.

Jacqo led Morning Dove, shivering, to the fire.

"Are you okay?" Raven ran over to her sister.

Morning Dove shook her head no. "It hurts when I pee."

"You're hot." Raven smoothed Morning Dove's hair off her sweaty face. "Are you chewing the herbs?"

"Yes," Morning Dove said as Lusio walked up. He smoothed Morning Doves' hair off her face and kissed her forehead. "Try to rest. We need to leave at first light."

Raven looked up at him. "We'll see how she is in the morning." Lusio gave her a long look, then turned and walked away. Morning Dove bit off another piece of the bitter root, chewing. She took a drink from the waterskin, then lay on the ground, curled next to Raven. Strong Eagle gently pulled the rabbit skin blanket off Aponi and covered them. Raven looked up, meeting Strong Eagle's eyes. He nodded in understanding and joined the brothers by the fire.

First light found Raven and Strong Eagle by the stream.

"Here it is," she said. "I knew I saw it." Walking over to a patch of small white flowers with soft yellow buttons in the middle, she reached down and picked a bunch. "This will help her fever." They refilled waterskins and headed back to the camp to see Lusio pacing.

"We need to go." Lusio removed his bandana, wiped his face impatiently, then wrapped it back around his head. "Andre? Jacqo?"

Strong Eagle shrugged.

"I found these by the stream." Raven showed Lusio and Morning Dove the flowers. "I'll put some in your waterskin." Raven lay the plants on a small, flat rock and chopped them. "Here, chew these now." She handed a few to Morning Dove, putting the rest into a waterskin. "The sun will make tea. These flowers will help your fever." Raven tucked her small knife into her pouch and smiled at her sister. "And the root will help where it hurts."

Morning Dove nodded and took the flowers. She took a leaf off one and put it in her mouth, chewing. "Thank you."

Raven lay her hand on Morning Dove's forehead. "You're still hot. How do you feel?"

"It hurt less when I peed this morning."

"Can you walk?"

"I think so. It helps to keep moving." The sisters looked up as Andre and Jacqo walked back into camp and dropped Mountain Mike's things on the ground.

Lusio, arms folded over his chest, looked at the pile and the brothers.

"We can use these." Andre took out the musket and tomahawk.

"What about the pelts?" Jacqo asked. "They'd be good for trading. You'll need something to trade when you get to where you're going."

Andre nodded. "Doesn't feel right." But he packed them on Willie. "Let's go."

FIFTEEN

It had taken most all day to reach the bottom of the mountain. Morning Dove rubbed her arms, shivering in the night air as Jacqo got a fire going. "All of our sleeping furs were on the travois." She looked up as Raven brought the rabbit fur blanket and wrapped it around Morning Dove's shoulders. "Here, you and Aponi can share this tonight. It'll help a little. How do you feel?"

Morning Dove shrugged, tightening the blanket around her and Aponi. With guilt, she looked at Jacqo, who rubbed his injured shoulder against the cold. "A little better."

Strong Eagle and Andre returned from the woods carrying two rabbits and a string of fish. Soon, everyone sat around the fire, rabbits roasting on a green stick and trout sizzling on a rock. "There's a creek on the other side of those trees. We can fill our waterskins."

"Oui." Jacqo gathered the skins and disappeared into the trees.

"It's only going to get colder." Lusio went over to an oak tree nestled between two pines and reached down, gathering a handful of acorns. "Too early for these to fall. A hard winter is coming, and once the heavy snow comes, we won't be able to get across." He looked up as the screech of an owl sounded in the distance.

Raven looked alarmed, holding her hands over her belly. "What will we do?"

"Tribes have settled in the mountains by the big river." Andre shrugged. "Some friendly, some not."

Lusio threw more wood on the fire, then nodded to the mountains. "Bear people. They might help us."

Aponi whispered good night to Etu, then snuggled next to Morning Dove under the blanket, and with the fire blazing, the group soon lay huddled on the ground in the glow of the fire, asleep.

Emerging from the last bend in the trail the next day, a whispering sound met them in the breeze. It was like the rushing water in a stream or rain greeting the leaves on a tree for the first time.

Lusio waved his hand. "Pando."

Moving closer to the sound, the trail opened to hundreds of golden trees on the plateau, leaves shimmering as they whispered in the gentle wind, white trunks shining in the sun.

"Pando," Lusio repeated. "When the wind blows the leaves of these trees, our ancestors are speaking to us. The grandmothers said they bring peace." He glanced over at Andre's hard stare, closed his eyes for a moment, then took a deep breath before continuing. "They welcome us and ask us to find that same peace within us."

Exhausted, the group stood in silence. Mesmerized by the sound, the feeling of the peace Lusio spoke of softened their faces as the promise of new beginnings washed over them.

"The trees begin as a single seed, then, over time, send out new shoots. Eventually, the underground roots weave together into a tribe, still one, yet branching out in all directions. The roots remain resilient, and new shoots always return, even after floods or fires. Nothing can destroy them. They are strong, knowing at the root of their being, they will always be one tribe."

Lusio listened to the leaves as they sang in the breeze. "At this moment, Spirit is greeting you. Like the trees, you must let Spirit move within you as well, and know even though terrible things have happened and everything feels shattered, deep within, the roots are mending and healing." Reaching up as if to touch the sun rippling through the trees, he closed his eyes and breathed deeply. "Every morning, be like the tree. Greet the sun with your feet bare on the earth. Feel the healing energy flow through your body like a river, greet the roots deep within, and then offer it to the sky, to the mountain tops, letting it ripple through and all around you. If you do this, in time, you will once again find balance, and have joy in your heart."

Raven kissed Strong Eagle on the cheek, squeezed his arm, and went to her sisters, taking their hands.

A soft breeze rose, lifting wisps of their hair into the air as they reached their hands together for the sky. Eyes closed, they let the warmth fill them, the rivers of light seeking out wounded places in their bodies and spirit, mending and weaving before traveling through their legs and into the ground, joining the roots underneath in gratitude to the welcoming of this new tribe. Taking a last deep breath, they separated.

Morning Dove smiled at Raven. "The pain is gone. Mama said one can always take their pain to the mountains, but I didn't understand."

Aponi whispered into Etu's ear, then held the doll to her, listening. She grinned up at her sisters. "Etu likes it here."

Raven tucked her hand into her pocket, feeling the energy of the talisman. "Thank you, Mama," she whispered as Strong Eagle wrapped his arms around her. She leaned into him and allowed waves of healing from the trees, the roots below, and the sun to penetrate the core of their being, to the new life within her they had created.

Andre stood in the trees, watching. Jacqo went to him, reaching out. "Andre, don't go."

Andre looked at him with pained eyes, then down as Aponi walked over and took his hand, her eyes filled with the innocence and love that was her. He looked back at Jacqo. "I don't know...." Andre squeezed Aponi's hand, stroked her cheek, then walked over to Willie, turning his back to them so they wouldn't see his eyes grow moist. The mule, also calmed by the whispering of the trees, snorted softly, blowing his warm breath into Andre's hands.

Seeing Aponi's sad face as Andre walked away, Morning Dove squatted down and hugged her. Jacqo reached out and took Morning Dove's hand. She stood, smoothing her hand through his hair and looked into his eyes. "You must trust." Jacqo leaned into her shoulder. He could feel her connection to the earth and the wisdom of her ancestors as it traveled through her and into him, and he knew he could never be without her.   Andre glanced back, then looked at the trail opening into the trees going east. He would never convince Jacqo to come with him. It was time to go.

"We'll rest here." Lusio looked up at a flock of birds flying from north to south. "Snow soon. We must leave tonight. The moon will guide us."

Strong Eagle reached out his hand to Raven. "Come."

As they disappeared into a blanket of trees, red and golden leaves fell around them, brushing their shoulders. Raven reached up, smoothing one out as it caught the white feather still woven into Strong Eagle's hair, her own strands wrapped around the shaft of the feather. "Thank you for believing in us, for not giving up."

Lifting her chin, he leaned down, letting his lips linger on hers, then deepened the kiss. Familiar feelings overtook them as they knelt together in the golden leaves. "My mate, my love." Strong Eagle swept together a pile of leaves, creating a soft mound. Raven pulled her dress off and lay cradled in the leaves, her hair fanned around her, the puma tooth shiny between her breasts. Strong Eagle knelt next to her, putting his hands over the bulge in her belly. "Our child."

"Yes." Looking up, she touched his face. "She will hold our memories and the memory of our people. Would you like to know her name?"

"Her name... she?"

Raven smiled. "When the moon caught the sun, I was afraid our babe had been harmed. Hiding in the cave, under your sleeping fur, I fell asleep and dreamt of an old woman. She held our child up to the firelight and pointed to a mark on her left foot shaped like a quarter moon. "Your daughter has been blessed by the mating of the sun and the moon. Her name will be Moon Dancer."

"Moon Dancer?" Strong Eagle's eyes grew big. "Blessed? Not cursed?"

"Blessed." Raven closed her eyes against a bright shaft of sunlight dancing through the trees. "Later in the dream, I saw us here, on this journey... and further on... I saw Moon Dancer. She was sitting on a large animal." Raven paused. "It looked like Willie, but bigger. There was a celebration happening. She had ribbons of many colors in her hair."

Strong Eagle lay holding his body next to hers.

"I didn't believe it until now." She turned to face him. "Thank you for finding me."

Wrapping his arms around her, he pulled her close and kissed her again. "Raven, my need is great. But I don't want to hurt you or our baby."

"My back hurts sometimes, and once I bled some." She looked up at him. "My need is great as well. How could our love harm our baby?"

He kissed her again, letting his hands run over her body.

"Gently," she whispered.

Andre smacked Willie on the behind, making the mule plod forward, snorting as Aponi tugged on his lead. Sounds of a rushing stream met them on the other side of scattered pines. As the mule drank, Aponi sat on the ground, pulling out a handful of grass. Leaning against a tree, Andre watched as she carefully counted twenty-one blades of the long grass. Knotting the end, she began to braid it.

"What are you doing, Aponi?"

"Making a new belt for Etu. Mama showed me how." She frowned as the grass slipped, making the braid come loose.

"Let me help you." Andre knelt and held the knot while she got the braid started. He enjoyed seeing her tiny fingers moving in and out of the weave, contrasting the assorted colors of the sweet grass. "Looks good, Aponi. Etu will like it."

"I dreamt about Chitto. He told me Etu needed a new belt and to not forget."

They looked up as Jacqo and Morning Dove walked up. She smiled down at Aponi. "Mama would be proud. May I join you?"

Aponi giggled while Morning Dove pulled grass and sat beside her, laying the strands in her lap. "What are you making?" Aponi asked.

"A belt like yours." The brothers watched as she knotted the grass, soon catching up with Aponi."

"Why did you count them?" Jacqo asked.

"Mama always said to braid in groups of seven." Morning Dove looked up and blushed at his gaze." The first bunch is to honor those who lived before us. And this bunch," she held up the middle, "are things that help us be good persons in this life. And the last is for our future generations, our children, and their children." Aponi looked over at Morning Dove, her giggle infectious.

Lusio watched the group from the edge of the trees. Leaning in, he could almost feel the hum of energy from the roots entwined below him. The healing power was like a salve, soothing the loss that scarred his soul with regret. *It may not have mattered, but I would have died protecting my family.*

Lowering himself to the ground, he closed his eyes. He felt blessed beyond measure with love in this lifetime, and now it was up to him to take this love with him and survive. He needed to remain strong. He would get the rest of the group to his childhood home.

Aponi finished her belt and pulled Etu out of the bag, careful not to drop Chitto's spirit arrow. Tying it around her corn silk doll, she held it up for everyone to see.

Morning Dove hugged her. "Aponi, how beautiful."

Opening the bag to put in the doll, Aponi stopped and held Etu up to her ear. She looked around, whispered in the doll's ear, then looked around again.

"What is it, Aponi?"

"Dada, he's sad."

Aponi walked a short distance and found Lusio sitting against a tree. Kneeling next to him, she touched his shoulder. He opened his eyes as she held out her bag with Etu and Chitto's spirit arrow sticking out. "Etu told me you were sad. Would you like to hold her for a little while?"

Lusio reached out, pulling Aponi onto his lap. "No, little one, she's yours. I'll hold you instead." Together they sat, the leaves whispering all around them.

Lusio stirred the fire in the fading light as Morning Dove and Jacqo prepared fish for the heated rock. The murmur of the leaves changed to a sharp, crackling sound as a cold breeze rose. Aponi snugged against Lusio and looked up. "If the leaves are Spirit talking to us, when they fall on the ground, where does Spirit go?" She ran her fingers over the belt she had made for Etu earlier. "How do our ancestors talk to us if the leaves are gone?"

"Ah, little one." Lusio pulled her onto his lap. "The leaves are born in the spring and spend the summer stretching for the sun. As they grow, they reach out to our ancestors who live in the stars and on the mountaintops, listening. In the fall, they gather all the warmth and wisdom from their ancestors and whisper it to us in the breeze as they fall. When the cold comes, they fall to the ground and go into the roots of the earth, remembering the life force that gave them energy. And then, when spring comes, more leaves can be born. This is the Sacred Circle of life."

Aponi put her ear to Etu and listened, then asked. "Where do the butterflies go when the leaves fall? Don't they get cold?"

"Like leaves, they start as bundles of mystery. Then, one day, they emerge into the sun with colorful wings, informing the world of all the joys and possibilities before us. Much like you, my little one."

Aponi stared at him with unblinking eyes.

Lusio sighed and continued. "When the cold comes and the yellow leaves fall, the butterflies find homes in the pines, whose branches and needles keep them warm."

"Ohhhh..." Aponi hugged Etu and laid her head against Lusio's chest.

"Look," Andre called out, pointing towards the mountains.

In the distance, two bears walked across the valley, disappearing into the trees. Lusio looked at the mountain, then back in the direction the bears went. "They are looking for a den to sleep in for the winter."

"They sleep all winter?" Aponi asked.

"Yes. And like us, when the bears sleep, their dreams tell them what will come when they wake in the spring."

Aponi stared, eyes wide. "Like the leaves?"

A sudden gust of wind came up. The air filled with leaves fluttering to the ground in random patterns.

Aponi stood, reaching out her hands, letting them brush her as they passed. "Dada, how do they know where to go?"

Lusio chuckled and stood, looking to the leaves for the answer. "They don't. Leaves trust the wind to carry them to the right place and at the right time. They exist in the moment with the buoyancy of the air."

Strong Eagle and Raven emerged from the trees, faces flushed. A smile passed between Morning Dove and Jacqo as Lusio, with Aponi at his side, walked toward them in greeting.

"Strong medicine here." Lusio brushed his hand over his daughter's cheek. "Are you well? It will be a long walk over the last mountain we must cross. There may be snow."

"I'm well, Dada. I rested in the trees."

Lusio looked up at Strong Eagle and then back at Raven. "Good. We'll eat, then rest until the moon is high in the sky. We need to be over the top of the mountain by sunrise."

Jacqo went to his brother, who stood outside the group, a distant look on his face. "You're leaving, aren't you?"

Andre looked at his brother. "Please come with me. Bring Morning Dove. They can all come and start new. If the snow comes, passage over that mountain will be dangerous.

Is it worth it?" Andre nodded to the trail which wove east through the trees. "Please... this is a better way."

Jacqo looked over at the fire, catching Morning Dove's face, bright with laughter as she talked with her sisters, her gaze turning to a question as she met his eyes. His heart knew that their and his destiny lay on the other side of the mountain.

Andre watched emotion flood his brother's face and accepted he had lost this battle. "I'll be on my way." He looked at Jacqo, the last hope for a change of heart fading. "The roots Lusio spoke of, I need to find mine. Ours."

Jacqo went over to Willie, untied him from the tree, and whispered in his ear. "You've been a good friend, Willie." He patted the rump of the mule, then led him to Andre.

"Take Willie." Jacqo handed the rope to his brother. "And the tools. You'll need them."

"Won't you come?" Andre asked again.

"No," Jacqo said, head down. "I'm sorry."

Andre remained quiet, his jaw tight and quivering.

"Promise me if it doesn't work out, you'll come and find us?" Jacqo whispered.

"Promise." Andre nervously twirled the hair from his long beard around his finger. "Remember, wherever I am, there will always be a place for you."

"I can't believe this is happening." Jacqo wiped a tear from his eye.

"But it is." In silence, the brothers packed up the mule for the last time.

Jacqo returned to the group, shoulders slumped. "Andre's leaving." He nodded to the path between the trees, the ground now covered with leaves. "Going east... he'll take Willie." They all looked up at Andre as he walked over. "I wish he would stay." Jacqo's voice broke.

Willie snorted, scuffing the ground with his hooves, restless to move. Andre checked his pack, tightened the lead on Willie, tugged on his hat, and turned to the group. Aponi stepped forward and took his hand. Andre gazed into her eyes, full of questions yet also understanding. He picked her up, hugging her for a long moment, then set her down. She tugged on his pants and held out Etu. Fighting back tears, he took the doll, held it close, then squatted down and tucked it into her bag. He leaned in, kissed her cheek, and then stood, going to each person to say goodbye.

"How can we thank you?" Strong Eagle asked.

"You already have," Andre said. "Take care of her." He nodded towards Aponi.

"We will." Strong Eagle dug into his pouch, pulling out a fishing line and hook and handing it to Andre. "May you always find food."

"Thank you." Andre put the gift into his pocket and embraced his friend.

Raven and Morning Dove stood, looking with uncertainty at him. Raven got the rabbit skin blanket she had made, offering it to him. "You will need this."

Andre glanced at the mountain behind them and then back to her. "No. I thank you, but you'll need it more." Morning Dove joined them, and he put his hands on their shoulders, staring into their faces. All he could see was Aiyani and, not thinking his heart could break more than it already had, pulled the sisters into a hug.

Then he approached Lusio. The two men stood, taking each other in. Andre reached out his hand. Lusio took it.

Jacqo secured the tools and pelts on Willie's back, then handed Andre a waterskin.

"Keep this," Andre said, taking the ax off the mule. "You'll need it crossing the mountain."

"I'll walk with you for a while," Jacqo said.

"No, you have a mountain to cross and a village to find." Andre studied Jacqo's face for a moment, then nodded. "I'll be on my way." He turned, taking Willie's lead.

Jacqo reached out and touched Andre's shoulder, who turned and swept his brother into a hug. He cupped Jacqo's face in his hands as if taking in all the details, never wanting to forget. Then, Andre stepped out of his brother's embrace, tipped his hat to the group, and turned, walking away, Willie plodding behind. The group stood, watching as the duo faded into the trees.

Jacqo paced back and forth. "I don't know how to do this," he murmured under his breath. "How can I let him go? How can he leave me?" He stood looking into the trees, hands shaking as he ran them through his hair. Strong Eagle walked over, offering a waterskin. Jacqo took it and drank as he stared into the empty distance. Turning, he watched the sisters at the fire, smiling as Aponi gently brushed the dust from Etu's head.

Family.

He stared into the empty trees, then turned back to the sisters. Morning Dove stood, combing her fingers through her hair, holding his gaze.

What if something happens to him... We've always had each other... I can't... Jacqo shook his head and kicked at a pebble on the ground.

Lusio stood. "Time to go," he called, shadows of the coming night descending around them.

"Let me wrap your ankle, Dada." Morning Dove went to Lusio's pack and pulled out a strip of leather. As she wrapped it around his ankle, it was like she pulled in the healing from the trees' roots and strengthened him with each turn. "There."

Lusio stood and walked around the fire, a gentle thoughtfulness filling his face, eyes moist with tears. "Thank you, daughter. Your mother's healing touch lives within you."

"You're welcome." Morning Dove hugged him. "Ready?"

Aponi tucked Etu into her bag and slipped it onto her shoulder. She looked up as two large orange and black butterflies floated amidst an occasional leaf floating in the air, dancing in circles as they hovered around her outstretched hand. The butterflies swept in, brushed her fingers, then flew back toward the aspen trees Andre faded into. She watched them fly away, then turned and walked over to Jacqo. Reaching up, she took his hand. The two stared together at the path in the trees.

"Need to go," Lusio repeated.

Jacqo turned and met Morning Dove's smile, tentative now. Looking toward the east one last time, he knelt so Aponi could climb onto his back, then walked over to Morning Dove and took her hand. Together they fell in step behind Lusio.

Watching, Raven touched the talisman in her pocket. "A'ise Mama! A'ise!" She looked up at Strong Eagle.

"It is good." Strong Eagle nodded.

SIXTEEN

In the early hours of the morning, just at daybreak, a fine mist began to fall. Strong Eagle lifted Aponi and put her on his back, squeezing her feet around him. Exhausted, she lay her head against him, arms wrapped around his neck. Lusio turned and looked back, feeling his heart lighten, as it always did at the sight of her.

"Ice forming," Strong Eagle said. "Might see snow."

Morning Dove saw the worry on Raven's face. She took her hand and then glanced over at Jacqo. He'd been silent since Andre left, often turning to look behind him as they ascended the mountain.

By afternoon, the icy rain became snow. Exhausted from walking all night, they were relieved to see a series of caves and rock overhangs. "There's a cave big enough for all of us over here." Lusio pointed to the rock overhang above. "We'll have protection from the snow." Several tiny squeaks preceded a pair of weasels running out as he disappeared inside.

"We need wood," Jacqo said.

"Shoulder?" Strong Eagle asked.

Jacqo moved it around in a circle. "Not bad."

Minutes later, the crack of wood filled the air as Strong Eagle and Jacqo split fallen logs. The sisters gathered brush, pinecones and twigs. Soon, a fire blazed under the overhang. Lusio emerged from the woods, dragging long branches from pine trees and laying them on the cave ground.

"Maybe I can scare up something." Musket in hand, Jacqo walked into the forest. Strong Eagle watched, a frown on his face, and looked over at Lusio. "I'll go." A bit later, the sound of the musket being fired suggested success. Soon they walked back into camp, carrying two cottontails and three grouse.

"Fired the musket up into the tree, flushed 'em out." Jacqo gave Morning Dove a blank look. The sadness in his eyes broke her heart. "Gotta clean and reload this. Don't know when we'll need it." He leaned the musket against the cave wall.

"Creeks not far." Strong Eagle pulled out his extra hook and fishing line from his pouch. "Let's fill the waterskins and get some fish."

Lusio and Jacqo helped Morning Dove prepare the game as Raven gathered up the waterskins and followed Strong Eagle. He looked back at the snow falling in her hair, her beauty filling him to his core. She met his gaze and smiled. Tempted to linger, at Raven's shiver, Strong Eagle pulled the last fish out of the creek, and with full waterskins, they returned.

Lusio gathered and rolled large rocks into the fire as the meat and fish sizzled. Later, as night fell, the men rolled the heated rocks into the cave for warmth. The group snuggled in the soft pine needles with full bellies and slept.

Sounds of tree limbs breaking woke them just before dawn.

"What is it?" Raven sat up, looking around the cave. "Where's Aponi?"

Snow covered the ground, the air thick with white flakes.

"Heavy snow breaking the branches." Lusio turned to the girls. "Stay here and build up the fire. We'll find Aponi." Following her small footprints toward the creek, Lusio disappeared into the woods while Strong Eagle and Jacqo, with musket in hand, headed in the opposite direction.

Lusio stopped at the sight of Aponi coming out of the woods.

"Dada, who is that man?"

"Aponi! What are you doing out here? Man?" Lusio turned and looked. "I don't see anyone."

"He was big, Dada."

The sound of the musket reverberated through the air, making the leaves shake and pinecones fall. Strong Eagle came out of the trees.

"Bear," he said.

Jacqo emerged, smoke drifting out of the end of the musket. "Didn't get it. Too fast, but I chased it off."

Lusio knelt, pulling Aponi towards him. "What did the man look like?"

Aponi's eyes grew large as she held her arms stretched out wide. "He had long gray hair and black eyes."

"Where did you see him?"

"I was in the trees," she said. "When I stepped out, he was there, and then he was gone, into the air."

Lusio's face filled with alarm, then became thoughtful. "It's too dangerous to keep going." He looked at the snowfall, getting heavier. "But help may be near."

"Help?" Strong Eagle asked.

"Might be an old friend. He'll show himself when he's ready."

"He? I saw a bear..." Jacqo trailed off.

"Aponi has always seen things others can't. If it's who I think, he'll be back." Lusio glanced into the woods. "Glad you didn't shoot him."

"What was it?" Raven and Morning Dove asked in unison as the group joined them at the fire. "Is it gone?"

Jacqo put the musket down and looked around at everyone, shrugging. "Guess so."

"Aponi, are you okay?" Morning Dove asked, scolding her little sister. "Always wake someone, okay?"

A frown spread across Aponi's forehead. She walked away from the group and took Etu out of her bag, whispering in her ear.

"She's doing it again," Morning Dove said to Raven.

"Walking in her sleep?" Raven asked.

Morning Dove nodded. "Let's keep her between us tonight."

Lusio went into the cave and pulled out the big rocks, rolling them into the fire. "Cold tonight... snow's not stopping."

"I'll hunt," Jacqo said. "And get more wood."

"Stay close." Lusio watched Jacqo walk away, musket and ax in his hands. "Go with him." Strong Eagle followed his friend.

Afternoon found the group huddled around the fire, the snow getting heavier. It drifted around trees but stopped short of the cave, small scattered puddles from the heat glimmering in the firelight. Rubbing her arms, Raven turned to Morning Dove. "Let's make a pit to smoke the extra meat and fish." She nodded at the skins lying on the ground. "We can stretch those out by the fire. Might have enough for another blanket soon."

Raven picked up a stick and dug a small hole, smoothing it into a circle. They gathered smaller rocks to line the pit, then added coals from the big fire, twigs and wood. With a small fire blazing, they pulled small pine boughs from nearby trees and layered them with the flattest rocks they could find over the fire.

Strong Eagle and Jacqo returned, holding grouse and rabbits in the air. "Got these." Jacqo took them to the edge of the circle, the snow turning bright red as he prepped the meat for the fire. "Still need more wood."

Morning Dove knelt next to him. "I'll do this. You get the wood." She smiled as her sisters joined in. Together they prepped the meat, then stretched the skins out to dry near the fire. As night fell, the snow continued falling, their feet sinking deeper whenever they left the cave.

Lusio looked worried. "Let's get some rest."

Morning Dove woke to the sound of wood being thrown onto the fire, grateful for the heat. She felt the stones around the edge, hot when they went to sleep but cold now. Turning over, she felt the space where Aponi lay and then sat upright.

154

"Is Aponi over there?" Morning Dove whispered to Jacqo, who came back into the cave, rubbing his arms against the cold.

"No, I don't see her."

"Raven, is Aponi with you?" Everyone sat up, looking at the space next to them.

"Oh no." Morning Dove looked out at the snow. "She was right next to me."

"We'll look for her," Lusio said, stepping out of the cave with Strong Eagle.

"Dada…" Morning Dove called, but they didn't hear her as they walked into the blowing snow.

Lusio took a piece of rope out of his pack and bound his wrist to Strong Eagles. "We must stay together." A long while later, they returned to the rest of the group, standing at the cave entrance, waiting for them. Brushing the snow off, Lusio shook his head no. Both men stood near the fire, shivering.

"Oh no," Raven cried. "What can we do?"

Jacqo looked around, pulling back a long branch from the nearest tree. "Let's make a torch. We can take turns looking for her. She can't have gone far."

Aponi came out of her spell, disoriented and shaking from the cold. Unable to see in front or behind her, she felt for her doll, comforted by Etu's soft face. Tucking the bag under her arm so Etu wouldn't get cold, she took two or three steps forward, then tripped over a large branch and rolled down the hill towards the creek, stopped from falling in the icy water by a large tree. Feeling the trunk, she found a hollow in the tree and crawled in. Peering outside, all she saw were the crystals of blowing snow, sparkling yet blinding. Curled around her doll and Chitto's spirit stick, Aponi fell asleep.

Strong Eagle and Jacqo, torch in hand and bound by rope, walked toward the creek, calling Aponi's name. But the sound of their voices was lost in the blowing snow, and the torch sputtered.

"We better head back," Jacqo yelled. "We're losing the torch."

"Aponi!" Strong Eagle called out once more. Aponi lay curled in the tree an arm's length away.

"I'm sorry," Jacqo said to the sisters, inconsolable, as they stepped back into the cave. "You can't see or hear anything out there."

156

The day wore on with no sign of Aponi. Morning Dove and Raven sat in the dark at the back of the cave, an occasional anguished sob being heard. Lusio held the torch in the fire, but it wouldn't stay lit. "There's nothing we can do but pray."

Raven stood at the cave entrance, the talisman clutched in her hand, staring into the blanket of snow which defied the night. "Mama, help us. Help Aponi." She had no tears left, only a feeling of hopelessness. The sound of footsteps drew her attention. "Aponi?" Raven ran to the other side of the fire just as a large shadowy figure appeared in the snow. "Dada," she yelled. When she turned back around, the figure was gone. On the ground lay Aponi.

SEVENTEEN

"What?" Lusio yelled, the rest of the group on his heels.

"Aponi." Raven went to her sister and tried to pull her up, but Aponi lay limp on the ground. "Help, Dada."

Lusio scooped Aponi up in his arms. "She's freezing. Get the blanket."

Raven and Morning Dove removed Aponi's clothing back in the cave, then wrapped her in the blanket. Lusio sat near the fire with Aponi in his arms. "Gather around. Protect her from the wind."

"Etu is gone." Morning Dove looked around the fire where they had found her.

"We'll make her another doll," Raven said. "But Chitto's spirit arrow..."

Aponi lay in Lusio's arms, her breath becoming more even as she warmed. "Etu..." she whispered.

Morning Dove looked at Raven. "We must find Etu. It's the only thing that has gotten her through."

"We can't go out there," Strong Eagle said. "Aponi has us. And she's safe."

"You don't understand." Morning Dove got up and walked to the cave's outer edge, looking out. Sighing, she turned. "Etu means everything to her."

Day blurred into night, and the group, one by one, found a spot to rest. Lusio bound Aponi's arm to him and lay down next to Morning Dove. Jacqo stood, a lone figure, the fire reflecting light and shadow on his face. He gazed into the fire, searching for answers his soul didn't have. He turned to a hand on his back. Morning Dove took his arm and stared into the flames with him.

"If you need to follow Andre, it's okay." She looked up, smoothing the hair off his face, sweaty from the heat of the fire.

"I've been with him every day of my life. I don't know what to do." He picked up a piece of wood, throwing it on the fire. "Would you come with me?"

Morning Dove turned to face him, taking his face in her hands. He closed his eyes against the touch. "No. My journey is with my sisters and my father. And with you if you choose to stay."

Jacqo stood in silence, rooted to the spot.

She left one hand on his face and placed the other over his heart. "We are of the same tribe, no matter if you stay or go. But your head and heart must agree, or you will never find joy. I will honor your decision."

He leaned down and kissed her. It was the kiss he had dreamt of. The softness of her lips gave him the answer he needed. "I choose you." Together they stood, arms around each other, staring into the fire.

"Look." Morning Dove pointed to a long piece of moss hanging off a piece of wood, glowing bright red, framing the shape of a face. "It's Andre."

Jacqo watched in disbelief as the face and beard shape shifted into a blur, then disappeared into the flames. It was as if Andre was right there. And then gone. Was he alright? Calling out for help? Jacqo felt he might implode with unanswered questions, but his mind became numb as he shivered in the cold. He looked down at Morning Dove's face, somehow still peaceful after all she had been through, and berated himself for not being a stronger man.

"We're going to be out of wood by morning." Jacqo took a piece of wood off the dwindling pile and threw it on the fire.

"Maybe the snow will stop soon."

Jacqo didn't respond. He looked to the sky as the snow continued to fall and thought: *Snows too deep, it'll be days,* but said instead: "We'll figure something out." They both turned and looked in the cave at Aponi's voice calling out for Etu.

"Get some sleep," Jacqo said.

Strong Eagle lay awake, arms wrapped around Raven. He knew they were in trouble.

What would father do?

Raven stirred. Letting his hands rest on her pregnant belly, he felt the fear creep into him. It was he who had insisted on going south.

Father would never show fear. I must not either.

Raven mumbled, restless in her sleep. Her mother had come to her in a dream. As morning light crept into the cave, she struggled to stay asleep and dreaming.

"You did well, daughter. Continue to pray and to trust," Aiyani said in her dream. "Help will be here soon."

"Help?" she whispered. "But Mama, why didn't my prayers help you? Did I not pray hard enough?" On the edge of waking, Raven's hand sweat around the talisman as the rest of her shivered.

"Daughter." Aiyani faded into the trees as she spoke but looked Raven in the eyes. "No one knows what another person's journey is. That is between them and Great Spirit.

162

Yet when you pray and trust with a true heart, a path opens before you for the highest good, even though you don't understand it at the moment." Her mother's voice grew softer.

"Mama! No, don't go," Raven mumbled in her sleep. "I need you. Mama..."

Strong Eagle shook her. "Raven, are you okay?" She woke and told him about the dream.

"Lusio said the same thing when Aponi saw a man in the woods, that help may be near." They stood, walking to the outer edge of the cave, where she squatted. "Raven...?" Strong Eagle pointed to the snow, yellow with streaks of red.

"I've passed blood before." Wiping a tear away, she looked up at Strong Eagle. "I miss Mama so much."

Back in the cave, everyone stirred. Morning Dove helped Aponi into her dress, then wrapped the rabbit skin blanket around her, her hands shaking in the cold.

"Etu," Aponi whispered, looking around.

"Etu brought you back to us," Morning Dove said. "Then she had to go back into the forest for a little while."

"Is she coming back?" Aponi's voice caught.

"She has Chitto's spirit arrow with her. He will keep her safe." Morning Dove looked up at Jacqo's worried face.

Aponi sat down next to Morning Dove. "And the tree."

"Tree?" Morning Dove asked.

"I fell, then crawled into a tree. She'll be safe there."

Jacqo squatted down and pulled Aponi's chin up. "Morning Dove is right. She'll be back." Then, with ax in hand, he was already out of the cave and into the trees when Morning Dove caught up with him. "There's a tree down by the creek with a hollow in it."

Lusio stirred the fire, thoughtful as he watched them disappear into the trees, each step sinking into the snow, marking the path they took in his mind.

A little while later, Jacqo came out of the woods with an armful of wood, Morning Dove close behind. "Splits easy in the cold," he said, stacking it near the fire. Aponi stood at the cave entrance with a vacant look, staring past them into the woods.

"Look who I found." Morning Dove handed Aponi the bag she had hidden behind her back. "She was waiting patiently in the tree."

"Etu, you came back." Aponi hugged Morning Dove and then ran into the cave to show Raven. "She came back."

Jacqo's heart filled at the sight of Aponi's face, and the sound of laughter coming from the cave.

"You did a good thing," Morning Dove said. "Thank you."

Jacqo held her gaze, which reminded him of why he was here, in this place, with these people. "There is always something to be grateful for," he said.

As the day wore on into night, everyone settled into a simple routine of keeping the fire going, conserving food, and staying as warm as possible. Lusio stood at the entrance, looking out. "If it stays clear, maybe tomorrow we can try to clear a path and get down the mountain." But as he spoke, it started snowing again. "We better get fish before dark."

Snow grew heavy again as night fell. Fish lay in the smoking pit, and the group gathered around the fire. Strong Eagle's voice penetrated the silence with their familiar chant:

Heya Heya Heya Heya Heya Heya Ho
Heya Heya Heya Heya Hey Ho.

As his voice filled the cave, Lusio felt his heart swell when he heard his daughters join in, the sweet sounds of their harmonies flickering off the cave walls. It was like angels singing. The last time he listened to this sacred chant, sung to thank Great Spirit and ask for grace, Aiyani had been at his side. Out of habit, he reached down for her hand, his body jolting at the empty space. He listened, their voices like a salve in his heart, and joined them. Soon the energy filled the cave, drowning out the sounds of the storm, reminding them that as the roots of the trees, they were one, and together they were strong.

Jacqo sat nearest the fire, watching faces and shapes form in the fiery flames, then disappear. He wondered if the dance of the fire reflected their lives and if they would survive. Staying present in the immediate need, none of them had given voice to the danger they were in. The sound of Morning Dove's voice, in perfect harmony with the rest, reminded him to pray and trust, letting each moment lead to the next and then the next. It spoke to his soul, connecting him to lifetimes of knowing and loving. With all he had to offer as the man he was, he would fight to get them off this mountain, but if their journey ended here, he was at peace. He put one more piece of wood on the fire, then lay on the ground and listened as they sang:

Heya Heya Heya Heya Heya Heya Ho
Heya Heya Heya Heya Hey Ho... ooo

During the night, the snow stopped, but drifts piled all around the cave. Lusio lay looking out the cave entrance when he felt the rope tug that bound him to Aponi.

"Dada," she whispered. "The bear is here."

EIGHTEEN

Lusio untied the rope, nudging Jacqo as he crawled to the edge of the cave. He peered over the snowdrift near the entrance. A large black bear was walking into the woods. Raising his hands, he made the sound of an owl, fluttering his fingers to draw the sound out. The bear stopped as if to listen, then kept walking, his hind end brushing snow off the limbs as he passed through the trees. Lusio repeated the sound. The bear stopped, raised his nose to the sky, sniffing, and then disappeared. Lusio turned to the rest, who looked at him with sleepy eyes. Picking up a piece of wood from the dwindling pile, he tossed it on the fire. "Help will be here soon. Let's build up the fire." He went over and looked at the food cache. "Eat. You'll need the energy to get down the mountain."

"What? Who?" Strong Eagle asked, looking from Raven to Jacqo and then back to Lusio.

"Trust." Lusio stirred the fire, then opened the food cache. "You'll see."

The fire blazed, melting the drifts of snow that piled up overnight. Everyone sat near, sharing the last of their food.

Jacqo stood, staring into the woods. "Listen."

In the distance was the sound of something being drug on the snow.

"Back in the cave!" Jacqo picked up the musket, standing on the inside, out of sight. Strong Eagle and Lusio stood at the cave entrance, watching. Moments later, two large men, wrapped in furs, appeared on the trail, dragging a travois filled with blankets.

Lusio stepped forward, shaking the hand of the man in front. "It was you."

The man studied his old friend, then nodded. "We came as soon as we could."

"Come, warm yourself." Lusio led the men to the fire. "This is Bear Heart, Chief of the Weenuche."

Jacqo, wary after the encounter with Mountain Mike, leaned his musket against the cave wall, staying close to it as the rest of the group stood staring at the strange men. Aponi came forward and held her doll out. "This is Etu."

Bear Heart looked down, studied her, and burst out laughing, the sound echoing through the trees. He knelt in front of Aponi and, still chuckling, leaned down and whispered into Etu's ear, then held his down to the doll to listen.

"You have a good friend here." Bear Heart sat back on his haunches. Aponi stared at him, eyes not wavering, then turned and stood next to Lusio. The second man pulled blankets and robes off the travois, handing one to everyone.

"Our camp is at the bottom of the mountain," Bear Heart said. "You will be welcome there." He turned to Lusio. "It has been a long time, my friend... many, many moons. Last time I saw you, you were a boy, warning us about an attack."

Lusio told him about finding Lone Elk's tribe and how they took him in. "This is Lone Elk's son." Hearing his father's name, Strong Eagle came over. "And the girls are my daughters."

"Wife?" Bear Heart asked.

"No." His jaw tensed as he told them about the massacre.

"Ah, the Spanish. Creeping into the mountains. Loco..."

The second man grunted something, and Bear Heart nodded. "This is Tavaci. He doesn't speak."

Laying the last fur on the travois, Bear Heart held out his hand to the sisters.

"Raven," Strong Eagle said, "can sit on the travois with Aponi." Raven protested, but at his look, she sighed and sat, opening her arms as Aponi snuggled next to her.

"Can you walk?" Lusio asked Morning Dove, who nodded yes.

"And your ankle?" She asked.

"It's better. I wrapped it earlier."

The men made quick work of clearing the small camp. Bear Heart and Tavaci picked up the ends of the travois and led the group down the mountain.

NINETEEN

Lulled by the steady, gentle bouncing of the travois and warmth of the fur, Raven felt Aponi's head on her shoulder and wondered how it would be to hold her child. She looked up at branches layered with glistening snow, occasionally loosened by the vibration of feet crunching, making the snow sprinkle down on them. Her hand drifted down to the talisman in her pocket, calming her fears. She had told no one about the bleeding or pain in her back or how it worried her. But now they knew. Eyes closed, she drifted with the sound of the footsteps, feeling pockets of snow as they brushed her face.

Jacqo studied the backs of Strong Eagle and Lusio as he and Morning Dove walked behind them. He couldn't understand how Andre didn't see this tribe as their family now. Sadness overwhelmed him. Whenever he imagined footsteps behind him, he turned, only to see an empty trail. *Will I ever see him again?*

Hours later, with only patches of snow on the ground, the fire and food cooking smells greeted them. The men stopped at the bottom of the mountain, helping Raven and Aponi off the travois.

"This way," Bear Heart said. They passed through a grove of pines with an occasional oak snuggled in and walked into a clearing. The group stopped and stared. A village, very much like their old one, lay before them. Sounds of chatter filled the air as children played. Women looked up with curiosity from basket weaving, and men sat near the fire, sharpening sticks. In between the teepees, strips of pemmican hung from poles on forked sticks, drying.

Aponi stared at Bear Heart. In her mind's eye, she saw the bear shape-shift into a man and dissolve into thin air. The unexplained truth lay in her heart, but no one believed what she saw except for Dada. She tugged on his pants, whispering when he leaned down. "Dada, is he going to turn into a bear?" Lusio looked up and caught Bear Hearts' eyes, a smile passing between them.

"Not here, little one." He chuckled at her look of disappointment. "He only does it when the forest calls him."

"How does the forest do that, Dada? Is it like the butterflies?"

Lusio looked to the sky for the answer, then turned at a touch on his arm.

"How long has she had the gift of sight?" Bear Heart asked.

"Since birth. We've taught her to keep it to herself, but sometimes it happens without her realizing."

"She's safe here." Bear Heart squatted down to Aponi. "It's true what you saw, but let's keep it our secret, okay?"

Eyes big, Aponi clutched the bag, holding Etu tighter, and nodded yes to the big man.

He smiled and stood as an older woman approached them in a fringed buckskin dress adorned with quills and colorful beads. "My wife, Chipeta," Bear Heart said.

She smiled and nodded at Lusio, smoothing long, gray hair off her shoulders. She looked at Raven and walked over to her, lightly touching her growing belly. Chipeta motioned for Raven to follow her. Raven looked up in alarm, first at Strong Eagle, who stepped closer and then at her father.

"She will help you find comfort and give you a place to rest. Go." Lusio said.

Raven hesitated, her eyes darting from Chipeta to Lusio and back. Lusio nodded, watching as Chipeta took Raven's arm and guided her toward a nearby teepee. Raven stopped and motioned to Morning Dove to come with her, then looked to Chipeta for approval, who returned a warm smile and a nod. Morning Dove joined them, and the three women disappeared inside.

Jacqo stood back, taking it all in. All he could think about was Andre. Was he okay? Did I do the right thing? He knew he couldn't make it back over the mountain, and now they were in warmer terrain, his feet hurt. He looked down at his threadbare moccasins, then at the plentiful leather goods around him. Would they let him make a new pair? Lost in thought, he didn't hear Bear Heart walk up to him.

"You need new moccasins," the big man said. "You're in pain. Show me your feet."

Jacqo pulled the moccasins off for the first time in weeks, the leather pulling the skin off his red, swollen toes, covered with blisters, now oozing blood.

"Frostbite." Bear Heart motioned to the group of men gathered around the fire. Soon, two young men were helping Jacqo into a teepee, leading him to a buffalo hide on the ground. Sighing in relief, he lay down on it. He looked up as a young woman came in, carrying a basket of water, cloth, and another basket of herbs and salves. She knelt at Jacqo's feet, at first touching them softly and then pressing harder until he winced. At the point of pain, she began to massage above where it hurt, inviting blood flow back into his feet little by little. He closed his eyes, letting the bliss of being touched come over him. Gently, she sponged his feet with cool water, then dried them.

The young woman pulled out a tin in the basket of herbs, holding it up. "Osha." She rubbed it on his swollen feet, then wrapped them with layers of cloth. Feeling powerless to resist, he opened his eyes. He met her stare as she continued massaging him, up and down his legs, reaching under the worn fabric of his pantaloons. Noticing it pleased and stimulated him, she inched along the ground towards him, the smooth motions of her hands constant and persistent. Jacqo lost all sense of time and space as the difficulty of the past years washed away, taking with it the loneliness that had become familiar, like a friend. He closed his eyes, letting go, and drifted as if in a dream.

Strong Eagle made his way over to the men sitting around the fire, sharpening their digging sticks. Asking to join, men and boys soon stopped what they were doing and watched as he made delicate cuts in the wood, a snake emerging.

Lusio sat with Aponi leaning against him. It occurred to him Bear Heart had separated their group without him even realizing it. At that moment, Chipeta came out of the teepee where Raven and Morning Dove were and ducked into the teepee where Jacqo lay. Sharp scolding words sounded as the young woman came running out, tugging her dress down. On the other side of the fire, she turned, glaring at Chipeta, who stood holding the tin of salve in her hands.

"Tavaci," Chipeta called, nodded to where Jacqo lay, then returned to Raven and Morning Dove. Before stepping in, she stopped and turned, exchanging a meaningful glance with Bear Heart. None of this was lost on Lusio. Everything they were doing was purposeful. What did they want from them?

Strong Eagle handed the carved stick to a young boy, then got up and stepped into the teepee. Jacqo was pale, with a vacant look on his face. He looked up at Strong Eagle, tears forming in his eyes. Soon they rolled down his cheeks, and he lay an arm over his face. Strong Eagle covered him with a blanket and sat beside him, watching as Tavaci finished binding Jacqo's feet. Without saying a word, Tavaci turned and rummaged through a pile of leather, bringing out a large piece. Smoothing it on the ground, he put Jacqo's old moccasins on it and used his knife to trace a pattern. Without looking at or attempting to communicate with the men, Tavaci sat and worked until he pulled the last piece of sinew through, finishing the moccasins. He stood, placed them next to Jacqo, and left.

Morning Dove looked up as Chipeta came in, holding up the tin. "Osha." Morning Dove stood and sniffed it, making a face. "Root of the bear – good for what hurts," Chipeta said.

She motioned for Raven to turn on her side and began rubbing the salve into her low back. Raven groaned sighs of relief. Chipeta continued, pulling the balm down onto Raven's hips and legs. When Raven turned face up, Chipeta

178

frowned, placing a hand on Raven's belly. "Bleed?" Raven glanced at Morning Dove's surprised face and nodded yes.

"Nita," she called out. Soon, a young girl poked her head in. "Bring hot water and the basket of herbs for tea." She turned to Raven. "You need to rest. The tea will strengthen your belly to hold the baby. And this," she held up the tin, "will help where it hurts." Raven smiled her thanks as the young girl returned. Chipeta took a wooden mug out of the basket, poured the hot water in, and tossed in a handful of herbs. She turned to Morning Dove as Raven sipped the tea. "Show me your feet."

Morning Dove took off her moccasins, surprised to see her feet red and mottled. "Lay down." Chipeta massaged the salve into her feet and legs, then covered them with a cloth. "Rest with your sister." Standing, she put wood on the fire, and as warmth filled the teepee, she looked down and smiled. Both girls, curled into each other, were sound asleep.

Bear Heart handed Lusio a mug of tea, then looked down at his feet. "We'll make you some moccasins." Lusio looked at his friend, a flutter of warning that he couldn't identify rising from deep within. "You can share the teepee with your family." Bear Heart nodded at the teepee where

Raven and Morning Dove rested. "Jacqo can stay with Tavaci."

"Thank you." Lusio studied Bear Heart as he walked away, trying to make sense of what could be amiss.

Chipeta walked over, offering Aponi her hand. "Come, meet the children." Aponi looked up at her father and, at his nod, took the woman's hand. "This is Nita," she said, walking over to the young girl, drawing pictures on the ground with a stick. "She has a doll too."

As evening shadows fell, everyone came together around the fire, holding wooden bowls of stew. Raven looked up as a young girl offered her flatbread from a basket, smiling as she took a piece. It seemed only yesterday she was in her village, sitting with her community and sharing food. Strong Eagle came out of the teepee, Jacqo leaning on him. The sisters looked at his bandaged feet and the pain on his face. Strong Eagle led him to the group, helped him sit, and got him a bowl of stew. Jacqo took it but just sat with it in his hands, staring at the fire.

Morning Dove squeezed Raven's hand, then went over and sat by him. She reached up and touched his shoulder. "Eat, Jacqo. Then you can rest in our teepee." Looking at her blankly, he accepted a piece of bread dipped in soup. He stared into the fire, then across at the young woman who had been in the teepee with him earlier. She looked at Morning Dove, then looked back at him and smirked.

Strong Eagle went over to Raven, pulling her into a hug. "I'm going to stay with Jacqo tonight."

"Is he okay?" She asked.

"I don't know." Strong Eagle shook his head. "His feet are bad. And he's saying things that don't make any sense. I've never seen him this way."

Raven leaned up and kissed him good night. "You are a good man." Smiling, she caressed his cheek and followed Morning Dove into the teepee, where Aponi lay asleep on a buffalo hide. Morning Dove put wood on the fire, and both girls curled up with Aponi, soon sleeping.

As the evening grew late, Lusio observed Bear Heart standing in the shadows, whispering to Tavaci and then pointing through the trees. Tavaci nodded and left. Lusio walked over to Bear Heart, startled at the sudden presence of another. "Thank you for helping us. We might have died up on the mountain."

"Yes, I know." Bear Heart was silent for a moment, contemplating, then motioned for Lusio to follow him. "I want to show you something." An almost full moon shone down on the path leading through the trees, dancing with the shadows of the pines. Emerging onto a hillside, Bear Heart pointed. Grazing was a herd of wild horses. Tavaci stood nearby, prodding them to stay in the rough wooden enclosure.

"We raided a Spanish camp and took the horses." Bear Heart looked at Lusio's face. "Most likely, they stole them from someone else anyway."

Lusio counted the horses but lost count at ten. "What are you going to do with them?"

"Gentle them. Learn to hunt while riding. It will make it easier to move when we need to. But for now, we need to keep the horses hidden. Those Spanish soldiers don't forgive easily."

"What happened to Tavaci?"

Bear Heart shrugged. "When he was a boy, he was kidnapped by renegades. It was a full moon before we found him, huddled in a cave not far from here." A hard look came over his face. "He got away but hasn't spoken or made a sound since. We got him back, but he'll never be the same. We take care of our own."

Lusio looked up at him. "The same thing happened to me. Several moons ago, I left to guide traders over the mountain, and renegades were waiting for us." Bear Heart remained quiet, listening. "Then the massacre happened, and I wasn't there."

Bear Heart looked long at his friend and then lay his hand on Lusio's shoulder. "I'm sorry." Lusio turned and stared at the horses. Tavaci looked over and met his eyes. A gentleness that belied whatever the soldiers had done to him met his gaze, and he wondered if he had escaped a similar

182

fate. Lost in thought, Lusio was surprised at Bear Heart's voice.

"There aren't many of us. We want you and your family, even the white boy, to join our tribe." Bear Heart waved his arm toward the horses. "We are growing, but we need help. You were always loyal to us. We trust you."

Lusio, filled with fatigue and an aching body, tried to take it all in. He knew Bear Heart was right. They could stay. But his heart yearned for his homeland, and he wanted his mother and sister to know his daughters. He gazed at the horses, the moonlight reflecting off the horse's mane as the wind lifted it in the breeze. Aponi would love these horses, but the Zuni also had horses. He knew the travel was hard on Raven. She thought she had hidden the pain from everyone, but he had seen it and the streaks of blood in the snow.

"Can I think about it?" Lusio asked.

"Yes. Rest now. We'll have new moccasins for you tomorrow." Bear Heart clapped Lusio's back. "We can do good things together, you and I."

The two walked together back to the camp in silence. They shook hands before Lusio stepped into the teepee. The handshake had been genuine, and he believed Bear Heart, but he couldn't shake off the deeper warning that nagged him all day. His heart softened at the sight of his daughters sleeping peacefully for the first time in weeks. Lusio secured the flap on the teepee. Should Aponi walk in her sleep, she would remain safe inside. Wrapped in the buffalo hide, Lusio listened to the soft sounds of his daughter's breathing and drifted into a dreamless sleep.

184

TWENTY

Raven jumped at the sound of scratching on the side of the teepee. Her heart raced, memories of the massacre tangled with sleep.

"Raven. Morning Dove," Strong Eagle whispered.

Opening the back flap of the teepee, she looked over and saw Morning Dove sit up.

"What's happening?" her sister whispered.

"I don't know. Come with me." Together they stepped out to Strong Eagle's worried face.

"It's Jacqo. He's sick with fever. I can't wake him."

The girls followed Strong Eagle, passing Tavaci as he ducked out of the teepee. Morning Dove took one look at Jacqo and called out. "Tavaci. Get Chipeta."

Jacqo lay writhing where he lay, shivering and soaked with sweat. Morning Dove looked frantically around the teepee and grabbed the basket of cloth used to bind Jacqo's feet. She sat next to him, wiping his face and neck. He opened his eyes, but her face swam in front of him, and he cried out, shrinking back in fear.

"Jacqo. It's Morning Dove."

He calmed at the sound of her voice, reaching out his hand to touch her.

"I can't see," he whispered.

She took his hand, then lay beside him, letting her body warm him.

Raven held the flap open for Chipeta, who rushed in. Kneeling next to Jacqo, she felt his forehead, then smelled the sweat on her fingers, wrinkling her nose. Moving down to his feet, she removed the binding. The blisters on his feet oozed greenish, foul-smelling liquid. Standing, she went to the door, called out to Nita, then turned back to the sisters. "He's been cursed."

Bear Heart ducked under the flap, carrying a basket of water, followed by Nita with baskets of herbs and fresh cloths. Chipeta spoke to Bear Heart in a language the sisters didn't understand, an angry tone in her voice, gesturing with her hands. Bear Heart looked at Morning Dove, his expression turning grim, then left.

"You need to leave," Chipeta said to Raven. "It is not safe for your baby."

Raven looked up at Strong Eagle, waiting for her, and took his hand. "What is happening?" she asked, stepping out with him.

"She was with him yesterday." He nodded to the girl standing by the fire, staring at the teepee. "I was sitting with the men, carving pieces of wood, when Chipeta chased her out. Then Tavaci went in and finished wrapping his feet." Strong Eagle took Raven's hand, leading her to the fire and handing her a mug of tea. "Something didn't feel right, so I went in. Jacqo was crying. I've never seen him in such torture, so I stayed with him." Raven reached out and took his hand. "During the night, he was restless, but this morning he started sweating and yelling out things that made little sense, so I got you. I didn't know what else to do."

Raven stared into the fire, mulling over what he said, her talisman clutched in her hand. "Chipeta said he had been cursed." The girl who tended to Jacqo inched her way to the teepee, pressing her ear to the leather wall. She didn't see Bear Heart come from behind. He grabbed her arm, pulling her away into the trees, shrieking.

Strong Eagle and Raven stared in surprise.

"Is she a witch?" Raven looked up at Strong Eagle. "What did she do to Jacqo?"

"I don't know. Jacqo's pants were unbuttoned when I went in, and he lay naked." He looked worried. "I covered him, but was I too late? If she mated with him..."

They looked up as Morning Dove came out of the teepee, crying. Raven ran to her sister. "What is it?"

"Chipeta made me leave." She leaned into Raven. "I don't know how to help him. Curse? Who cursed him?" Raven looked uneasily at Strong Eagle, then pulled her sister close.

Lusio came out of the trees, holding Aponi's hand. "What is it?"

Strong Eagle whispered in Lusio's ear, explaining what happened and his suspicions.

"We need to leave," Lusio said.

"Not without Jacqo." Strong Eagle glanced over at the sisters.

Bear Heart emerged from the path leading to the horses, pushing the young woman ahead of him, holding long strands of hair in his other hand. Shamed, she put a shawl over her head, but not before they saw a bloody patch on her scalp where hair had been yanked out. He pushed her away, yelling: "Yak quah!"

Lusio's eyes got big, then he turned away, motioning for the rest to do the same. Morning Dove glanced over her shoulder as the girl crouched a distance from the others, shawl now covering her quivering body.

"What did he say, Dada?" Raven asked.

"He declared her dead. We must not look at her."

Bear Heart met Lusio's stare before ducking back into the teepee. Chipeta was putting new bandages on Jacqo's feet, and Tavaci sponged his face and neck with cool water. Jacqo shivered, then opened his eyes. Unable to focus, he pushed his hands against them, shrieking as if he were being attacked. Bear Heart handed Chipeta the hair, and then he and Tavaci sat on either side of Jacqo, holding him down as

188

he sobbed. Chipeta divided the hair into two bunches and put one bunch in each of Jacqo's hands, squeezing his fingers over the hair.

Morning Dove crouched in her father's arms, distraught. "I don't understand." Lusio looked over at Strong Eagle. He didn't know what to say, so he just held her. The smell of sage and tobacco drifted out of the teepee as Chipeta and Bear Heart began chanting. At first, their voices were soft, then grew louder, only to float to whispers as Jacqo calmed and rose again with his sobs.

The sun moved from east to west as the chanting continued in waves until, at last, it ended with a screech. Chipeta came out of the teepee and threw the two bunches of hair into the fire, which exploded in a ball of flame before disappearing into the air, black plumes of smoke drifting into the trees. The young woman collapsed under the shawl on the other side of the camp.

Bear Heart ducked out of the teepee, took ash from the fire, then returned, smearing it in the palm of Jacqo's hands and on his face. He looked up at Lusio standing at the door. "Your friend will wake soon. He'll think he had a bad dream."

"And the woman?"

"My daughter will be okay. She was possessed, and now that which possessed her is dead. The baldness on her head will shame her. This will not happen again."

"How did she become possessed?"

"One moon ago, a stranger came into camp. He said he was born of an Indian mother and a Spanish father, but he wasn't of our tribe. He was charming. My daughter disappeared with him for three nights. The next day, she wandered back into the camp. We didn't see the stranger again, yet she hasn't been the same since."

Jacqo stirred and opened his eyes. "Morning Dove," Lusio called from the door. She came to her father and stepped into the teepee, kneeling next to Jacqo. She called his name, and he held out his arm, and she lay next to him. They remained silent, breath moving in and out of their bodies in unison.

"I had a bad dream," he whispered. "I saw terrible things. I didn't think I would see you again."

Morning Dove remained silent, smoothing her hands over his face and hair, his body relaxing at her touch. As his breath deepened, she deepened her breath to match his.

Outside, Lusio, Raven, and Strong Eagle sat close, immersed in whispered conversation.

"Bear Heart asked us to stay and become a part of their tribe. On the other side of those trees," Lusio nodded to the trail he had gone on the night before, "are horses they stole from Spanish soldiers. He wants to strengthen the tribe. In return, they will help us."

Raven looked at her father. "What about your homeland? Your sister? Your Mother?"

"We still have a long journey ahead of us. Chipeta can help you give birth to your babe, and Jacqo can heal. When I wandered into Lone Elks tribe, he welcomed me, and I became family. This may be a good idea. Aponi would love the horses. He looked around. "Aponi?"

They hadn't seen Aponi get up and walk over to the young woman who lay under the shawl. The woman tugged on the cloak when she felt Aponi's touch, then stopped, looking up. Aponi stood, holding her hand out to three butterflies, who flew in gentle circles around the two girls. A golden butterfly landed in the palm of Aponi's hand. She held it out to the terrified woman, whose hands shook as she held them out. As the butterfly brushed her palms, the soft wings left a trail of powdery yellow dust.

Raven and Strong Eagle followed Lusio to where Aponi knelt next to the woman.

"I'm sorry," the young woman cried.

"What is your name?" Raven asked, kneeling next to her.

The woman looked confused at the kind voice, then said: "Miakoda."

"Ah, Miakoda, She of the Sacred Moon. I am Raven."

The woman looked at her, then up at Strong Eagle and Lusio, pulling the cloak tighter around her. "I am ashamed."

Raven held the talisman in her hand, searching for the words her mother might have said. "The moon is a powerful thing. Everything has a dark and a light side, an evil and a good. Now you know the difference. May you always walk in the light, Miakoda."

Chipeta joined them, bringing a tin of salve for Miakoda's scalp. She smiled at Raven. "Thank you. My daughter has learned an important lesson."

Bear Heart met Lusio as he walked back towards his teepee, Aponi nestled in his arms. "We are good together. I pray you stay."

Lusio stood for a moment, watching his friend walk away. The bad feeling in him had washed away, and yet he knew even though this could be a good place for them, in his heart, he wanted to take his family home.

At the evening fire, young girls passed baskets of fresh flatbread to dip into bowls of stew thickened with amaranth. The women offered baskets filled with wild raspberries, gooseberries, wild onions, and dandelion greens. Jacqo, nestled between Strong Eagle and Morning Dove, ate in silence, bits of stew dribbling down his chin. He looked across the fire and met the eyes of the girl who had put a curse on him, knowing she looked familiar but unable to remember why.

Soft voices murmured as children grew sleepy in their mother's arms. Chipeta, carrying a basket, sat next to Raven. "You create designs with beads?" Raven nodded shyly, peeking inside the basket, her eyes wide at the tins of beads, colors she had never seen before. Next to them, bundled, were bleached porcupine quills. Raven looked up and touched the quill and bead design on Chipeta's dress, which glimmered in the firelight. Chipeta smiled at Raven's touch. "I can teach you how to work with these, and perhaps you can show me your designs."

Raven looked into Chipeta's gentle eyes. "On my wedding dress, I beaded a shining sun," she lay a hand on her chest, "and put it here, reminding me to honor the sun each day and always be open to love."

"I'm sorry about your tribe. You must miss your mother very much."

Raven lowered her eyes, her hand brushing over the pocket with the talisman. "Yes, I do. And my little brother, Chitto. We were peaceful and happy. I don't understand why those men wanted to hurt us and were so filled with hate."

"Each of us chooses the path we walk, or sometimes, I suppose, it chooses us. The only difference between evil and light is one's intention. Your wedding dress sounds lovely. What happened to it?"

"Our travois fell off the mountain with all of our things." Raven shrugged, looking away. "It left us with nothing."

"Perhaps tomorrow you can begin a new dress?"

Raven smiled. "Perhaps."

Lusio looked down at his new moccasins. They were snug and warm. Tavaci had approached him as the sun went down and offered them. He ran his fingers around the seam, the stitching even and flat. The moccasins would last a long time. He looked up as drumming started, mesmerized by the steady beat, feeling his heart calm. After a few moments, Bear Heart stopped and held up his drum, addressing the community.

"Many of you won't remember, but many moons ago, Lusio visited our tribe. He was a young traveler at the time but warned us of an attack that would happen that night. We were able to get our women and children to safety and defend ourselves. Because of him, it saved many lives." Bear Heart's voice resonated in the air, then stopped as he looked at each person around the fire. "Great Spirit has brought him back to us with his family. I have asked them to stay, to join our tribe. Together we can be strong and thrive." He looked over at Lusio. "He hasn't told me his decision yet."

"We appreciate all you have done. If you hadn't come, we might not have survived the mountain." Lusio looked around the circle. His family had blended into the tribe. "I will dream about it and inform you of my decision soon."

Bear Heart nodded and smiled. "In six moons, when the flowers bloom, many will come and gather to celebrate as Mother Earth begins a new cycle. It is then we honor the dance of the bear." He looked sideways and winked at Aponi, whose eyes got big. "When a bear wakes from his winter sleep, we celebrate this awakening by dancing. It marks the end of the cold and celebrates the renewal of Mother Earth. Bear gave this ceremony to our ancestors, and we honor new beginnings and the return of flowers through dancing."

Lusio looked around as Bear Heart resumed beating the drum, the steady rhythm reflecting the beats of their hearts and earth mother herself. He had seen the excited look on Raven's face as Chipeta shared her basket of beads and quills with her. But the call of his homeland was stronger. He would wait to announce his decision until Jacqo could wear moccasins and walk. Even though the curse had been removed, the young woman who cursed him continued to stare at Jacqo with a yearning that made Lusio uncomfortable. It would be best for all if he took his family away from here.

Days later, Lusio's heart lightened when he stepped out of his teepee to see Jacqo walk out of the trees, moccasins on. Jacqo, unaware of Lusio's approach, looked up at him, a vacant look still in his eyes.

"How are your feet?" Lusio asked.

Jacqo paused, searching for words. "Good." He walked over to the trees leading back to the mountain. "I don't think Andre is coming back. Do you think he is okay?"

Lusio walked with him, contemplating the question. "Yes. He will find your people. Then one day, he will find you again." Morning Dove stepped out of the teepee, a smile forming as she saw Jacqo.

"Soon," Lusio said. "We will go." He hoped over time Jacqo would heal. Hotda would help.

TWENTY-ONE

The following day, Lusio turned to the laughter coming from the woods. It brightened his spirits even more than the sun shining through the trees. He looked up to see Raven, belly rounder by the day, emerge. Chipeta was close behind, carrying a basket full of fresh herbs and long bunches of grass.

"Dada," Raven said, flushed. "Chipeta is going to show me how to use different grasses to make flatbread." She smiled up at Chipeta.

"You have a daughter with many talents." Chipeta ran her hand over Raven's long hair.

"And beautiful too."

Lusio looked past them at Chipeta's daughter, Miakoda, who wiped a tear off her cheek and turned, walking away. His heart ached for Miakoda, who yearned to be the daughter Chipeta wanted, and for Raven, who only wanted her mother back. He had yet to tell them his decision. Bear Heart and Chipeta welcomed them and provided them with new moccasins, dresses, and robes. He looked over at Strong Eagle, surrounded by men and boys who watched as he carved animals out of pieces of wood and new arrows for their bows. A touch on his arm startled him. He looked down to see Aponi slip her hand into his. She had yet to join in with the other children. Bear Heart tried to engage her, teasing that he might turn into a bear at any moment. But she stood back, unsure if she could trust him. Lusio saw all of it and knew he had made the right choice.

At the evening fire, Bear Heart approached Lusio. "Your family is happy here. I feel as if you are already a part of our tribe."

"You are right." Lusio looked around at the circle of people, chatting and laughing softly. "There is joy here. Jacqo is better, and Raven is strong. You and Chipeta have been very good to us."

"You will stay?"

Lusio wavered. "My mother is old, and I wish for her to meet my daughters. My childhood home calls me." Bear Heart was quiet. "I will talk with my family tonight, and tomorrow I will give you my final decision at the morning fire."

"That's all I ask." Bear Heart stood and walked away.

Later, Lusio tucked Aponi in bed, then called everyone into the teepee. Jacqo hesitated, unsure if he should come in. "Please." Lusio gestured to Jacqo, then the door.

"Bear Heart is asking for my decision." He looked around at the group, quiet with anticipation on their faces. "We're comfortable here and welcome. But my sister and mother would welcome us as well, and you would know your blood." Lusio studied his daughter's faces. "I would like to go, but while the rest of the journey won't be as hard, it is long."

"How long, Dada?" Raven asked.

"One half-moon or more."

"Are you sure we will be welcome there?" Strong Eagle asked, putting his hand on Jacqo's shoulder.

"Yes, you and Jacqo will be welcome." Strong Eagle held his gaze, then looked at Jacqo, who remained silent. Lusio was more convinced than ever that Jacqo needed to be away from here. Miakoda often looked for ways to be close to him, sometimes walking in front of Morning Dove, blocking her from speaking to Jacqo. He turned. "What do you think, Morning Dove?"

She looked at her father, then at Jacqo. "I wish to go, Dada."

"Jacqo, what do you wish?"

"This is my family now. I wish to remain with you." He reached out and took Morning Dove's hand.

"We could build a travois in case Raven or Aponi find walking difficult." Strong Eagle said.

"Do the women in your childhood home have beads and quills?" Raven asked.

"Yes. Very colorful." Lusio smiled and cupped Raven's face in his hand. "Your talent will be treasured there."

"I believe if we don't go now, we will never go." Strong Eagle looked around the group. "This is a small band. Could they come with us?"

Lusio looked at Jacqo, uneasy at the thought. "Possibly, but it's not likely they would come. The Nuche is a large tribe and lives in small bands except when they come together for celebrations." He glanced at Aponi, asleep on the fur. "And the horses, they could not bring them."

"Why?" Strong Eagle asked.

"They're not gentled yet, and it would be difficult to move horses without the Spanish knowing, whom I'm sure are looking for them." He reached his arms out, pulling them together, hands on each other's shoulders. "We will sleep and let our dreams inform us," Lusio said. "In the morning, we will talk again. And I will tell them our decision."

"Okay." Strong Eagle turned to Jacqo. "Stay in here with us tonight."

The following morning found the camp shrouded in fog. Lusio opened his eyes to see everyone else gathered around him, awake.

"We have decided." Raven took Strong Eagle's hand and faced Lusio. "We wish to go to your childhood home."

200

She smiled at the relief on his face. "I wish to meet my grandmother and have my child with your people."

Lusio smiled. "Our people. I will inform Bear Heart we will leave today."

Lusio stepped out of the teepee to see Chipeta and Bear Heart sitting near the fire, deep in conversation. They looked up at Lusio's approach.

"We have decided." Lusio started to sit next to them, then remained standing at the worried look on their faces.

"Before you say anything," Bear Heart said. "There is something you must know."

Lusio looked Bear Heart in the eyes. "Speak."

"Miakoda is with child." Bear Heart took Chipeta's hand, tears streaming down her cheeks. "She claims the child is Jacqo's."

TWENTY-TWO

Lusio remained silent, his face stoic as his heart raced at this news.

"She must marry," Chipeta cried. "Or be shamed."

"Before we arrived here," Lusio started, turning to Bear Heart. "You told me Miakoda had gone away with a man for three days. The child is his, not Jacqo's. We have been here less than a moon. The child is not Jacqo's."

"It is impossible to know for sure." Chipeta pleaded. "You will leave and let my daughter face this shame?"

"I am sorry." Lusio looked at the couple, the deep lines in their faces showing their years. "You are welcome to come with us. But we will leave today. And Jacqo will go with us." Bear Heart shook his head and put his face in his hands as Chipeta stood, looking at Lusio with desperate eyes.

"I'm sorry," Lusio said. "My children wish to know their grandmother, and I want to return to my tribe. We will prepare to leave." Lusio walked back to the teepee but stopped at the strained sound of a whisper. He looked over as Tavaci stopped Chipeta, taking her arm.

"I wish to take Miakoda as my mate." Words, broken and strained, stumbled out of his mouth.

Stunned, Chipeta stared. "You speak."

Tavaci stood, looking over Chipeta's shoulder at Miakoda. "I love her." Miakoda blushed, looking down. "I will protect her."

Chipeta looked up as Bear Heart joined them. He cupped Tavaci's face in his hands and turned to his daughter. "Do you wish this, Miakoda?"

Miakoda looked past Lusio to Jacqo, who stepped out of the teepee. With a flicker of disappointment, she turned to Bear Heart. "Yes. I wish to be Tavaci's mate."

Chipeta hugged her daughter, then Tavaci.

"We are honored," Bear Heart said, taking his wife's hand.

Lusio stepped past Jacqo and ducked into the teepee. "Get your things together..." he started, then looked around. Everything was packed, and the teepee was clean, as if they'd never been there. Fresh wood lay next to the fire pit, and the sleeping furs were rolled up and stacked against the wall.

"We all have a pack and a waterskin." Strong Eagle looked at Lusio. "We will make a travois if we need one." One by one, they stepped outside the teepee, surprised to find Bear Heart and Chipeta standing next to a travois loaded with sleeping furs and a large cache of food.

"You will always be welcome here," Bear Heart said. "Go in peace."

Lusio took his old friend's hand and held his eyes. "Thank you. And know you and your family are always welcome in my tribe."

Bear Heart looked at Aponi, who had taken Lusio's hand, and smiled. Kneeling next to her, he tucked a stone into her hand and whispered first in her ear, then in Etu's. Eyes wide, she leaned down and listened for Etu's whisper. At her giggle, the air in the camp lightened.

TWENTY-THREE

Days later, Lusio stood on the hard granite top of a mesa, pointing to three rivers in the distance, branching off in different directions. "Totah."

"Totah?" Raven asked.

"Where the rivers meet," Lusio said.

Strong Eagle put the travois down and stood with the others, a feeling of peace coming over them as the sun drifted to the west. Rivers as blue as the sky sparkled in the waning light, surrounded by craggy cliffs of sandstone, their jagged peaks reaching for the heavens.

Lusio pointed to the rock formations, swirling colors of red and orange cliffs. "They are the guardians of the land, of the waters." A breeze made the leaves on the cottonwoods along the riverbanks shimmer. Lusio led the group down a narrow, rocky trail along the mesa's edge and across open land, stepping around sweet-smelling sagebrush and scrubby juniper. As the sun turned orange and the sky became shades of gray, he found a grove of pinyon pines next to a stream. "We'll stop here."

A fire blazed in the center, trout sizzling and sputtering on green sticks. Morning Dove and Raven lay sleeping furs on the ground and passed baskets of flatbread and greens from the food cache. As darkness engulfed the camp, bellies full, one by one, they drifted to the furs. Lusio lay next to Aponi, the rope joining them, and looked over at Jacqo, who sat staring into the fire. He had hoped Jacqo would brighten as they gained distance from Bear Hearts camp, but he had spoken little, and the vacant look was still in his eyes.

Jacqo studied the fire, searching the flames for Andre's face. Memories of the trek over the mountain were vague, and he feared he would forget what his brother looked like. Looking up through the treetops, he glimpsed a star streaking through the sky. *A sign?*

Thoughts floated through his mind, none lingering for more than a second or two. Lulled by the sounds of nearby crickets, he banked the fire and snuggled into the last sleeping fur. In a dream, he saw Andre at a crossroads, unsure which way to go. His brother looked back toward the mountains as if searching for something. Recognition filled Andre's face as Jacqo felt their eyes meet. Andre tipped his hat and then turned away, waving a hand over his shoulder as he continued following the trail east. The dream shifted, and Jacqo saw a woman's face framed by long, golden curls. She would be waiting for Andre at the end of the trail and become his wife. The woman radiated sweetness and joy, much like their mother. Waking for the first time since his brother left, a peacefulness filled him, and then, feeling sure Andre was safe, felt his body relax and drifted back into a deep, restful sleep.

The next morning, Lusio sat with Aponi on the stream's banks, the fishing line floating on the water. "Aponi," Lusio asked. "What did Bear Heart whisper to you and Etu?"

"He said if I was ever afraid and needed help, to call on the Spirit of the Bear." She checked her bag, stroked her doll's purple hair, then looked up at her father, holding out a stone. "And he gave me this."

Lusio held the stone up to the light, shades of pink and blue, threaded with copper which sparkled in the sun. "That's good advice, little one. Remember it." He put the stone in her hand, closing her fingers over it.

They looked up at the shrill call of birds. With their talons clasped, two eagles were spinning as they rode the airwaves towards the ground, only to pull apart at the last minute, spread their wings, and take flight again. The eagles flew in a spiral, one coming close to the other, only to swoop below and circle around, challenging the other. One eagle chased the other off. "What are they doing, Dada?"

"They are fighting over territory. One will stay, and one will go." Lusio stood and, taking Aponi's hand, walked to the edge of the trees, looking up at the mesa they had descended from the day before. On the ridge stood the figure of a man. He had an array of colorful feathers braided into his hair. The desert sun reflected on them, creating the illusion of wings flying as a breeze lifted them. Holding his hand to shade his eyes against the bright sun, Lusio tried to make out the face but was unable.

"We are being followed," Lusio told the group at the fire. "Let's go. Stay close to each other." They packed their things on the travois, filled their waterskins, and left. Occasionally Lusio would stop and turn, pretending to talk with Strong Eagle or Jacqo but discretely scanning the surrounding area in the distance, catching quick movements on surrounding mesas or across empty spaces, each time closer.

Sometime later, the sound of an arrow whistled through the trees, landing in front of Lusio. The head of the arrow buried in the ground at his feet. Motioning for the rest to stop, he pulled the arrow out of the earth and studied it. "Dine," Lusio said.

At that moment, three native men dressed in buckskin loincloths came out from behind nearby trees. They stood staring at the group, and then the tallest one, with feathers in his hair, spoke. "Where are you going?"

"Zuni." Lusio looked at the man with feathers braided in his hair, holding his stare. The tall man motioned as if he were drawing a boundary on the other side of the trees.

Hand on his knife, Strong Eagle stepped in front of the sisters. He looked over at Jacqo, who had the musket out of the sling. "What do they want?" Raven whispered.

"We are on their land. They insist we leave." Strong Eagle whispered, pointing to the rock formation in the distance. "They said we must go around the other side of that mesa."

Lusio stood silently appraising the three men. "We will go." He handed the arrow to the tall man and led the group to the other side of the mesa, aware their every move was being watched. "Aponi, get on the travois," he mumbled. "We must keep moving." She scrambled on, and the group stepped up their pace. As the sky faded from blue to orange, they reached the far side of the mesa, and Lusio signaled for them to stop. "We will camp here tonight. Someone needs to remain awake and watch."

"I will." Jacqo had already started gathering wood for a fire.

"At first light, we'll continue." Aponi leaned into Lusio, eyes closing as they ate a simple meal of flatbread and dried fish. Lusio took the rope out of his pack, tied Aponi's arm to his, then gathered her up and settled into their sleeping furs.

She had not wandered since they had been on the mountain, but he would not take any chances.

Morning Dove lay nearby, looking at Jacqo. He was different since he had been cursed. She didn't understand what happened in the teepee with Miakoda and suspected the others knew and weren't telling her. In their tribe, transparency was a way of life, and feeling left out made her uneasy. Her breath caught as Jacqo looked over, his eyes resting on her. Even though his face lit up when he saw her, he remained distant and quiet. Drifting to sleep, she wondered what their future held.

Jacqo sat near the fire with his back against a tree, where he could see anyone who entered the camp. As the night grew quiet, exhaustion claimed him, and he didn't feel his musket slip out of his hand and onto the ground. He awoke to a sharp poke on his arm. Startled, he reached for his musket. The moment he realized it was gone, shrill sounds of whooping filled the air, growing more distant with each second as the thieves ran into the night.

Lusio was at his side in an instant, Strong Eagle right behind.

"My musket..." He jumped up. "Who? What happened?"

"The warriors we saw earlier. They counted coup on you."

"What?" Jacqo asked, stunned into full awakening.

212

"They steal something of value and touch their enemy without harming them before running away. It gains prestige in their tribe and shows dominance." Lusio sat in silence as Jacqo took this in. Even though it was anger, it relieved Lusio to see a light in Jacqo's eyes for the first time in weeks.

"I'm sorry. I fell asleep." "Jacqo leaned his head against the tree. "What can I do?"

"You must get the musket back." Lusio looked at Jacqo, then Strong Eagle. "You can help him. Otherwise, we will be perceived as weak and will become a target."

"How can I help?" Strong Eagle asked.

"You become the tracker and find where they sleep. Take the musket back, touch them, and as you run away, make a victory cry. But you must not harm them."

Strong Eagle looked at Jacqo. "We'll go together."

"We will stay here until its done," Lusio said. "They are young and foolish. It will be easy to find them sleeping.

TWENTY-FOUR

The following night, the sisters watched as Strong Eagle and Jacqo smeared ashes from the fire on their bodies. Lusio studied the men. He took more ash, darkening their faces, and then tied his bandana around Jacqo's head, covering his light hair. "You've been tracking them and know where they sleep," Lusio said. "If you can't get the musket, you must take something of value. And remember, don't hurt them."

Raven came and stood in front of Strong Eagle. "Be careful."

His eyes softened at the worry in her eyes. Reaching out, he left a black mark as he caressed her cheek. Then, the two men edged their way around the mesa with the moon high in the sky. They waited for clouds to cover the moon before crossing open ground, weaving through spiky cacti and sagebrush to the opposite plateau where the three men had camped.

A narrow crevice in the cliff revealed footholds. Climbing the path to the top, they soon smelled fire and then, at the sight of flames, stood behind the pines, watching. The three men studied the musket, then took turns pointing it at each other, laughing. Angered, Jacqo took a step in their direction, but Strong Eagle grabbed the back of his shirt and pulled him back, holding a finger up to his mouth.

Soon bored with their antics, the three men settled around the fire, juices from the meat dripping down their faces as they pulled rabbit meat off the bones with their teeth. A loud belch announced full bellies, and two wandered to their sleeping furs. The tall man with feathers in his hair sat at the fire, the musket leaning against a nearby tree.

Strong Eagle and Jacqo snuck into the camp, coming to an abrupt stop as the tall man got up, threw more wood on the fire, then froze as if sensing their presence. He looked around in the darkness, staring straight at them without seeing, and then turned to the loud snort of the man sleeping closest to him. Shaking his head, he laughed as he sat down near the fire.

Reaching around the tree, Jacqo put one hand on the musket and, with the other, poked the tall man on the shoulder. Surprised, the man looked around, and as he jumped up, Jacqo gave him a push, his feathers a flurry of color above his head in the firelight. The tall man could not get his footing before Jacqo and Strong Eagle raced to the mesa's edge and scrambled down the side. At the bottom, Jacqo held the musket up to the faces of the startled men looking down at him and yelled his victory cry.

They ran across the open plain, whooping and hollering. Once across, Jacqo and Strong Eagle stopped and looked back. The three men remained on top of their mesa, watching. Giving a final victory shout, Jacqo held the musket in the air. Grinning, he led Strong Eagle as they ran around the rock formation and to the camp where the rest of the group sat waiting, sleeping furs rolled up and tied to their backs.

"Let's go," Lusio said. "Leave the travois here. Take whatever you can carry."

Strong Eagle bent over and scooped up Aponi, Etu and Chitto's arrow tucked under her arm, and the group set off under the light of the moon, almost full. They walked until the sun had risen high in the sky, reaching the first of the rivers they had seen from a distance days ago. "It's safe," Lusio said. The exhausted group stood under the shade of cottonwoods, gazing at the blue ripples on the water.

Strong Eagle stepped forward, dropped his loincloth on the ground, and broke the silence with a shriek as he splashed into the river. Looking over at Morning Dove with a blush, Jacqo dropped his clothes on the ground and yelled as he leapt into the icy water. Surfacing, the men grinned at each other. Victory felt good. The sisters dangled their feet in the water, laughing as the men flung handfuls of water at them. Lusio looked up from the fire, now blazing.

Aponi took Etu out of the bag. She stroked the doll's purple corn-silk hair and snugged the doll's new belt. "How's Etu today, Aponi?" Morning Dove asked.

Aponi whispered in the doll's ear, then looked up at her sister. "She's happy."

Later, around the fire, Strong Eagle and Jacqo's eyes were bright as they retold the story of recouping the musket. Lusio nodded with approval as Jacqo stood and showed how he grabbed his musket and gave the tall man a push at the same time. "Nobody steals my musket," he bragged.

"But he did." Lusio looked up at him. "Victory is sweet, but you must never take it for granted."

"I didn't hurt him." Jacqo sat back down, grinning sideways at Strong Eagle.

"Where is your musket now?" Lusio asked.

Jacqo looked at Lusio, scanned the surrounding ground, and looked up at Strong Eagle in a panic.

"Here." Lusio walked around the fire, handing Jacqo the musket. "In your eagerness to get in the river, you left it over there." Lusio nodded to the opening in the trees.

Sheepishly, Jacqo took the musket from Lusio, who, without expression, turned and walked away.

Morning Dove watched Jacqo across the fire. She felt relief at his smile but was still puzzled about what had happened at Bear Heart's camp. Longing for her mother, she leaned into Lusio. He wrapped his arm around her and leaned

218

down, whispering in her ear. "It'll take time, sweet one." He squeezed her shoulder. "Be patient." She looked up at him and then rested her head on his shoulder as she stared into the fire. So much had happened and now here they were, in an unknown land, going to a place where she knew no one.

"I laid the sleeping furs around the fire." Raven smiled at her sister.

"How much longer, Dada?" Morning Dove asked.

"If nothing slows us down, four or five sunrises." Lusio looked around at the group. "We're between Dine and Apache land but on an honored trading path. We'll be safe, but stay together and don't wander off."

"I'll sleep with Aponi tonight, Dada." Morning Dove took the rope from Lusio, tying it to her sister's arm. Lusio nodded, watching as Strong Eagle and Raven climbed into their sleeping furs across the fire, soon leaving Jacqo, the only other one awake.

"How are your feet?" Lusio asked him.

"Don't hurt much anymore." Jacqo threw a piece of wood on the fire and began banking it for the night. "I had a dream about Andre. I think he's okay. Might be getting married."

Lusio nodded. "Good."

"Did I do the right thing?" Jacqo asked.

"You followed your heart, as did he." Lusio looked up as a bat swooped down, snatching a mosquito out of the air. "That's all you can do."

"Can't sleep." Strong Eagle plopped down between them. "Lusio, tell us about your village."

Lusio looked at him for a moment and then smiled. "Soon you will say our village."

"What is your mother like?" Strong Eagle asked.

"Hotda is old now, blind. But she sees everything." He chuckled. "She's always been the healer for our tribe, even though she is the first to be blamed for illness, death, floods or droughts."

"Who would make such a judgment?"

"The Council of Priests." Lusio scowled. "A long time ago, many, many moons, long before I or even Hotda was born, Spanish soldiers came. Coronado was their leader. They attacked us, brought sickness and stole our land. They disrupted everything in the life of Zuni, who also suffered raids from Apache and Dine."

Strong Eagle and Jacqo stared at Lusio, listening.

"Zuni were shattered. Our tribe dwindled from these mysterious illnesses and attacks. We continued to grow corn, squash, and beans along the river but were always ready to go to Corn Mountain, where each family kept a home.

"Corn Mountain?" Jacqo asked

"Yes. It is a big mesa near our pueblo. There are only three ways to get to the top of Corn Mountain, none of them visible to the naked eye. There's a narrow trail for horses on the west and two paths between crevices on the north. We dug footholds and, once at the top, threw down a ladder so the children and elderly could get up. When rumors of an attack came, everyone went to the top of the mountain, and we pulled the ladders up. The soldiers couldn't figure out how we disappeared into thin air. We had prepared so we could stay up there for extended periods. Eventually, whoever attacked us would run out of food, get tired and leave."

"We are going to Corn Mountain?" Strong Eagle asked.

"Yes," Lusio said. "When I escaped from the men who captured me, somehow, I made it back to my childhood village along the Zuni river. Lolotea, my sister, told me that not long before, the Apache and Dine joined the Zuni and drove the Spanish out but remained living on Corn Mountain. She said they began farming along the river again and resumed making pottery, but stayed on the mountain for safety.

"But what about the soldiers who came to our village? Are they from the same army?" Strong Eagle asked.

"Yes. But without a leader, they became aimless and lost their way. They turned to evil," Lusio looked at the young men. "When one loses respect for the earth, they lose what holds their body in this world. The mind gets confused and grasps in desperation to survive. They forget that in the end, we are all one tribe, just as the trees teach us." He rubbed his arms against the chill of the night. "That's why each sunrise, we greet the new day with gratitude. And with each sunset, offer thanks for what we have been given. We take nothing for granted and seek permission from the earth before taking anything."

"The men who took my musket...."

"They wanted to show dominance but did not hurt you." Lusio paused. "Man wants to own the land but forgets the land owns them, so they battle over nothing. Change will not come soon, if ever." He looked at the sky, then at the men. "Rest now. It will be time to travel soon."

TWENTY-FIVE

The group walked along the winding dry wash leading south as light edged over the cliffs. Spiky purple flowers on long stems grew from the dry, cracked earth. Lusio scanned the horizon, then studied the ground, frowning at the scattered fissures filled with small pools of water. "Watch out." He pointed to the puddle. "We've had little rain, and it's too dry for this. Sometimes water collects underground and bubbles to the top, leaving a hole under the surface. Walking on it can make it collapse, and you'll fall in."

Raven took Aponi's hand, nervously stepping away from the puddle. She looked back with a frown as Morning Dove and Jacqo, who had lingered behind, ran up laughing.

"What's wrong?" Morning Dove asked.

"You should be listening to Dada," Raven snapped. She repeated what Lusio had told them, then turned her back on her sister with a stony silence.

"I'm sorry, we were just..." Morning Dove caught up with Raven, touching her shoulder.

Raven paused, took a breath, and turned, hugging Morning Dove. "I'm sorry. It just feels like every step holds danger in our new life." The group walked in silence, allowing the sun to melt the tenseness.

"What's that?" Aponi asked, pointing to a massive stone structure in the distance. The rest crowded behind her, looking.

"A great city once stood there," Lusio said. "It is the place of our ancestors."

"The Ancient Ones?" Raven asked. "Mama used to tell us stories."

"How did they build this?" Strong Eagle peered into the distance, hand shading his eyes. "It almost reaches the sky."

"The soil here is rich in clay, and we mix it with water and grass, then form it into blocks. Once dried, they are solid and can be stacked on each other. "They built this city where traders from many lands came. But over time, they pushed the earth beyond her limit, building bigger buildings and more roads in and out of the city. One day the rains stopped, and a great drought occurred. It became hard to grow crops. People were hungry, started fighting over the water, blaming each other and accusing members of the community of witchcraft. Newcomers, once welcome, were met with suspicion." He pointed to the dry wash they walked through. "Once, this was a flowing river carrying water to the city, but it dried up. Water is the source of life; without it, they could no longer exist here, so they left."

"Where did they go?" Jacqo asked.

"The Zuni remained on their land, as did the Dine and Apache, but many people who lived here scattered, joining or creating other tribes along the big rivers. Lone Elk's tribe, our tribe, were descendants of the Ancient Ones."

Aponi listened with Etu near her ear and then tugged on Strong Eagle's arm. He leaned down and smiled as she whispered in his ear. "Lusio, Aponi wants to know if we can go there."

"Yes, I'd like to see it too," Morning Dove said.

"We need to fill up all our waterskins, as there is no water there." Lusio scanned the group. "It's about half a day extra walking. Raven?"

"It's okay, Dada. I'm drinking the tea Chipeta gave me. It helps."

"Come on, Jacqo," Strong Eagle said. "Let's fill up the water skins."

The group walked in silence along the scrubby wash, and as they neared the first structure, Aponi stopped. "Dada, look." Aponi pointed to a snake rubbing along the rocks in the wash.

Lusio stopped, holding Aponi back. "The snake is preparing to shed his old skin. He rubs the scales on his body on the rocks to loosen them."

"Scales?"

"Yes, like this." He pointed to his fingernails and then hers. "We have them on our fingers and toes, but snakes have them all over. They grow another layer of scales under the old ones and then shed the old skin."

"Why, Dada?"

"The snake moves through the world much like rivers flow through the land. Rivers are constantly changing. Some days they are strong and full of energy. Other times they become clogged with debris and heavy with burden, grow sluggish, and water no longer flows, so it dries up." He pointed to the riverbed.

"But what about the snake Dada? It dries up?" Aponi walked forward, reaching for the snake.

"Aponi, no." Lusio jogged forward, catching her. "You mustn't go too close."

"Why, Dada?"

"Hear the sound the snake is making with its tail?"

She nodded, eyes wide against the rattling sound.

"The snake is telling you to stay away, warning you it will strike if you get too close."

"Will it hurt me?"

226

Lusio squatted next to her. "It could, but a snake only bites to defend itself. Some snakes have poison inside them, and we could become sick if they bite. So we give them space."

"Oh..." Aponi whispered in Etu's ear.

The group stood in silence, watching. The snake, little by little, moved forward as the old skin came loose around its head and then inched forward, leaving the old skin intact, lying on the ground. Aponi's eyes got big as the snake, born again with fresh skin, darted away.

"Why do they do that, Dada? Can I? Does it hurt?" Aponi asked.

Lusio chuckled and looked to Raven and Morning Dove for help, but they weren't listening. "Like the earth, the snake depends on the balance it finds as it moves along deserts and riverbeds. A snake can outgrow its skin or get wounded, but it always senses when to shed. And when the time comes, the old skin is released, as well as the burdens it carried. Look." Lusio pointed to the snake, which slithered down the dry wash and then up on a rock, basking in the sun. "See how the new scales reflect ribbons of color in the sunlight? Having let go of the skin that no longer protects, the snake can taste the energy of what's to come."

Lusio looked up at their blank faces and realized that while old stories have a place in one's spirit and body as a memory, the physical reality is gone with unfamiliar terrain.

With only the unknown standing before them, he understood their fear.

"It is a lesson for us," he said. "Sometimes, you must let go of the old so new skin can grow. It is a part of being alive. Like the river, we are always changing. As the old falls away, new stories can be told. Our ancestors teach us this. It can feel strange, and at times there might be a longing for the old story, which is why with each new sunrise, we pause and greet the new day with all its possibilities. Life will always pull us forward until we take our last journey, where we'll join our ancestors. But for us, today is not that day."

Aponi held her doll up to her ear, a frown forming.

"What is it, Aponi?" Lusio asked.

"Etu is worried she will shed her purple hair." Aponi stroked the doll's hair.

"It's true, Aponi." Lusio knelt next to his daughter. "Over time, our physical bodies change. Our hair becomes gray, like Bear Heart and Chipeta, or sometimes it falls out. But tell Etu it will be a long time before it happens to her."

Aponi whispered in Etu's ear, and then looked up at her father. "Thank you, Dada."

228

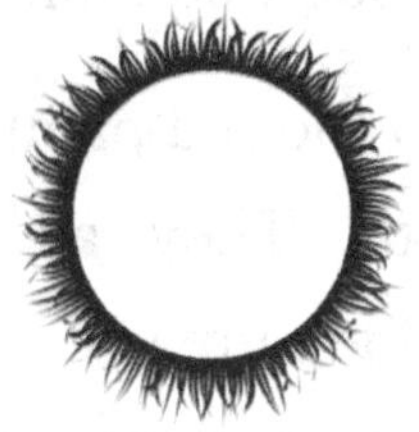

TWENTY-SIX

Minutes later, they stepped into the first giant structure. Morning Dove and Raven sighed in relief as they sat on a cool stone ledge, looking around them at the hundreds of abandoned rooms.

"K'ohanna me'oshe," Lucio waved his hand at the white cliffs surrounding them.

Jacqo scrunched up his face. "White house?"

"Yes, like the rocks. This is a sacred place and the center of our world," Lusio said. "Still, water is life; there is not enough water here to sustain life or a community." He pointed at the massive structure. "See how the doorways and windows are aligned to allow light to move through the entire structure?"

The group nodded, taking a step forward, spreading out to touch the cool, jagged rock, tracing the seams of dried mud and clay between blocks.

"The people who lived here were expert sky watchers. Using the sun, moon, and stars as a guide, they tracked moments in time and created ceremonies based on when the light aligned through the doorways and windows." He led them up a steep, grassy slope until they came to a horizontal overhang and pointed to the red painting of a crescent moon, a star and a handprint. They all crouched underneath, twisting their heads to look up at it.

"A long time ago, a star exploded when our ancestors stood in this very place. It was a star so bright it could be seen in broad daylight for the rest of their years. The storytellers say one of our ancestors, a star watcher, painted the star in its position to the crescent moon of that night. And then he signed it with his handprint."

"These were our ancestors?" Raven asked.

"Yes," Lusio said. "The same ancestors we honor in the first seven strands of a braid of sweetgrass."

Aponi held Etu to her ear, then tugged on Lusio's pants. "Can I leave my handprint here?" She whispered.

He smiled at his young daughter and repeated to the rest. "Aponi wishes to leave her mark, to let the next seven generations know she was here. She says it will remind them to remember us."

"We can make the marks of our journey," Raven said. "Our story can live on over time."

"That is possible," Lusio said. "But it will take at least one whole skin of water. Are you willing to be a little thirsty to do this?"

Aponi held out her waterskin. "We can use mine."

"And we can share ours with you, Aponi." Morning Dove said.

They went down to the bottom of the hill, where they found large sections of white rock. Jacqo dug the red dirt into a mound while Aponi tipped her waterskin, trickled water over it, then stirred it into a paste with a stick. Lusio helped Aponi bury her hands in the mud, then walked over to the rock wall. Lusio lifted her while Raven helped her position her hands to leave the perfect handprint.

"That's beautiful, Aponi," Raven said, watching as Strong Eagle carved a figure of each of them onto the rock. "Our family," she smiled, pointing at the figure, belly round with child. "I want to leave my mark as well." Raven and Morning Dove went over to the mound of red mud, burying their hands.

"This feels so good," Morning Dove said. "Soft and cool."

Lusio stood back, watching their story come to life on the rock wall. Sadness filled his heart Jacqo carved a figure looking back.

"It's so Andre will always know I watched for him." His eyes grew moist as he finished the carving, then started on another. He smiled down at Morning Dove as he carved two figures walking together, holding hands.

"It's late," Lusio announced, looking up at the sun. "Let's go.

The group stood together in silence for a moment, looking at their story.

"Even though we don't know what lies before us," Strong Eagle said. "I feel better. Thank you, Aponi." She grinned up at him.

Lusio led them through the dry wash to an even bigger structure. "Me'oshe co'ya."

"Beautiful house," Strong Eagle said, looking in awe at the hundreds of rooms lining the rock walls four stories high.

"This was the main gathering place, where ceremonies were held and trading was done," Lusio said. "Along the wall over there," he pointed to circular chambers sunk into the ground. "Kivas. This is where men would gather to pray, discuss politics or plan a hunting party."

"Women didn't go there?" Morning Dove asked, looking down at the stone walls, a bench built around the outer edge.

"For special occasions," Lusio said. "Look over here." They walked to a similar structure. It had an adobe roof and a ladder sticking out of an opening.

"Can we go inside?" Aponi asked.

"Not safe," Lusio said. "This is very old. The wood holding up the roof might break."

"Oh," she said, whispering in Etu's ear.

Raven put her hands on her belly and then leaned into Strong Eagle. Everyone was quiet.

"I feel our ancestors," Strong Eagle said. "I am grateful you brought us here."

232

"Dada," Raven said, looking up at Strong Eagle. "Would you bless our union? Bless our child?"

Lusio looked at her, opened his mouth, and then shut it.

"It's just you weren't there when we married. I want to receive your blessing, and that of my mother, in this place of our ancestors."

"Your mother was happy for you to marry Strong Eagle." His eyes grew misty at the mention of Aiyani. "We would sit at the fire and watch the two of you falling in love."

"I would like this as well, Lusio," Strong Eagle said.

Lusio looked at them thoughtfully. "Very well. Let's find a place to have a fire and settle for the night. We will gather in the kiva at sunrise."

TWENTY-SEVEN

Morning came gently to the canyons, new light weaving through the portals of stone, imagined wisps of ancestors in the shadows. In the kiva, the group stood in a circle, with arms outstretched in gratitude for the new day, as their soft harmonies rose, joining the whispers of the ancient ones.

Ah eh ta ho ta hey	*(A he! Arise! Arise!)*
Eh ta ho ta hey	*(Rise! Arise! Arise!)*
Ah ah eh ta ho	*(Ah eh Wake Up!)*
A ya he ta ne	*(Life is calling you.)*
Ah ah e ta ho	*(Ah eh! Wake up!)*
A ha he ta ne	*(Life is greeting you.)*
A ha a wey	*(Father sun God,*
	he is calling you.)
O wey to na wey	*(Father sun God,*
	he is greeting you.)

Lusio stood in front of Raven, her face cupped in his hands. Pausing, his eyes gazed at the rock formations around them, then he looked into her eyes. "Just as I see the faces of our ancestors, I see Aiyani in your smile, your tears... your beauty and grace. From the time you were a young girl, your mother and I watched your friendship with Strong Eagle grow. And now, you stand before me, asking for my blessing.

Do you, daughter, choose Strong Eagle as your mate and father to your children?"

"Yes, Dada. I choose Strong Eagle as my mate and father of my children."

Lusio turned to Strong Eagle. "I have watched you grow from a boy to a man. The beauty of your heart shines through as you walk the path of a warrior. Lone Elk would be proud of your strength in these challenging times and of the man you have become. You have always been a welcome member of our family. If my daughter chooses you for her mate and father of her children, then I am proud to call you my son."

Placing a hand on each of their shoulders, Lusio turned the couple to face each other. "I speak for myself and my beloved, Aiyani." He paused, listening as a morning breeze came up, whispering through the rocks. "And for Lone Elk and all the ancestors that witness us here today. Your union is blessed, and your child will be loved and cherished by all."

Aponi brushed her doll's purple cornsilk hair out of her face, whispered in her ear, and looked up at the couple with a grin. Walking over, on tiptoes, she gave Raven and Strong Eagle a kiss on each cheek. Morning Dove followed. Jacqo made like he was going to kiss Strong Eagle on the cheek, then laughed and pulled the couple into a hug, opening his arm for the rest to join.

"It is good." Lusio wiped a tear from his eye. "Time to go. We need to get to the river by sunset."

TWENTY-EIGHT

Lusio led the group out of the canyon. Scrubby pine and spikey cactus lay before them, with orange blossoms dried and scattered on the ground. One by one, they paused and looked back as the ancient city grew distant, wondering what life was about to bring them. He watched as they sipped from their near-empty water skins. "We'll be at the river by nightfall, but there's no water between here and there." In the distance, they could barely make out the green of the tall cottonwoods which lined the river. "So make your water last."

“Want us to run ahead and fill the waterskins?” Jacqo asked.

“Better to stay together." Lusio stepped around a thorny branch and froze as a snake darted out in front of him, moving sideways, tail up and rattling. The group halted behind him and watched as the snake slithered away, disappearing between the crevices of two rocks. Pulling a long stick out of a dead pine scrub, Lusio proceeded slowly, thrashing the brush, but no other snakes darted out. Satisfied, he motioned for everyone to continue.

As the sun moved west past the midpoint of the sky, Lusio climbed out of the dry riverbed, the rest following. Rainbow-colored mesas rivaled the blue of the sky, and the dry grass turned into juniper scrub and green cacti with long, thick arms reaching out and up to the sky, razor-sharp points glistening in the sun.

"Can we stop and rest?" Raven wiped the sweat off her brow. "Just for a short while?" Lusio nodded. Aponi tugged on Morning Dove's arm, then whispered in her ear.

"We'll be right back," Morning Dove said.

Lusio jogged over to her, giving her the tall stick. "Be careful."

"Okay, Dada." Morning Dove took the stick and called over her shoulder. "We won't go far."

TWENTY-NINE

"Aponi, look! Berries!" Morning Dove dropped Aponi's hand, ignoring the small cracks on the ground pooling with water. It had been many days since they had found fresh berries, and her mouth watered at the sight of the bush.

"Wait," Aponi said. "Dada said to be careful if we saw puddles."

Eager for the taste of berries in her mouth, Morning Dove ignored her sister and snuggled in close to the scrubby tree, tangled with vines of wild raspberries. Stretching tall, she grabbed a branch and pulled it down, laughing as a berry fell and bounced off her shoulder. Suddenly, the earth gave way.

She screamed as a gaping hole opened beneath her. "Dadaaaaaaa..." Grasping the branch, Morning Dove disappeared inch by inch into the dirt, her voice echoing through the air until it became muffled and then silent. At the sound of feet pounding down the trail, Aponi pointed at the sinkhole. In the middle, Morning Dove's arm stuck out, clutching the branch.

"Get back," Jacqo yelled, flinging himself on his belly. He crawled to the edge and grabbed Morning Dove's arm just as the branch snapped, raspberries flying like random pellets through the air. Lucio edged next to him, frantically scooping dirt out with his hands. Morning Dove gasped as he uncovered her face.

"I've got you," Strong Eagle called out from behind, holding Lucio's feet.

"Wiggle your legs, Morning Dove, like you're swimming." Lucio leaned into the sinkhole, the earth crumbling under his weight, and wrapped his arms around his daughter. "Pull!" Morning Dove slid free as they rolled into the bushes, their bodies a blur of motion, seconds from being drawn into the sinkhole.

Raven jerked Aponi away as they rolled by her, then gasped. "Dada! Snake!" Dazed and frantic by the upheaval of earth, the rattler struck out, biting Lucio before disappearing under the brush. Lusio looked at his arm, then up at Jacqo. "Get her to a safe place."

Morning Dove sobbed, tears streaking through dirt caked on her face as Jacqo led her away.

"Get up." Strong Eagle offered Lucio a hand, then saw the bite mark, reached under his arms, and lifted him.

"Dada..." Raven cried out.

Lusio stumbled, then held out his hands in front of him. "Can't see," he whispered, falling to the ground.

Strong Eagle hoisted him over his shoulder and called out. "Raven, pick a bunch of those long, flat leaves we saw on the other side of the boulder. Be careful. We don't know where the snake went, might be a nest."

Strong Eagle carried him around the rocks, where Jacqo held a trembling Morning Dove. Raven stood with an armful of leaves, torn. Both her father and sister needed her.

"Jacqo, we need a fire." Strong Eagle said. "Leaves, Raven." Strong Eagle's voice made her move, and she joined Aponi, kneeling next to them.

"He's been bitten twice." Strong Eagle pointed to bites on Lucio's arm and face. "Chew on those leaves. I'll suck the venom out, and we can pack the wet leaves around the wounds." He took out his knife and cut an X over the wound on Lucio's cheek.

"Is he going to live?" Raven's voice trembled.

"I don't know." Strong Eagle leaned down, sucked the venom out of the face wound, and spat on the ground. He rinsed his mouth, then repeated the same on Lucio's arm. Raven and Aponi took the wet, mushy leaves they had chewed and packed them around the wounds.

Strong Eagle looked over and saw a fire blazing under a rock overhang. "Need to get him out of the sun. Help me." The men carried Lusio next to the fire, laying him next to

Morning Dove, who, despite the hot day, sat huddled, shivering.

"I'll stay with them." Raven sat on the ground between Morning Dove and her father. "Are you okay?" Raven asked. Morning Dove nodded, leaning into her sister's shoulder.

Lucio opened his eyes briefly to the sound of his daughter's voices and reached out his hands, searching the air. "Where are you? I can't see."

"Right here, Dada." Raven held Lucio's head up as Aponi held the water skin to his lips, wetting them.

"Hard to swallow." Lucio gasped.

"His throat is swelling." Strong Eagle took leaves out of his mouth and smoothed them into a ball. Leaning over, he squeezed the liquid out of the leaves and into Lucio's mouth. "The juice of this plant will help."

"We need water." Jacqo gathered up the empty skins. "The river isn't far. I'll go."

"No," Morning Dove called out in a whisper. "Don't leave."

"We have to have water," Jacqo insisted, reaching down and smoothing his hand over Morning Dove's cheek. "I'll be careful. It won't take long." A frown creased Strong Eagle's forehead as Jacqo walked out of camp.

244

THIRTY

Lusio fell onto the bedroll, his back arching in spasms. Breath came in wheezes, and sweat streamed off his face as shivers coursed through his body. Each effort to draw in air took him deeper into a dream, back to their old village, where he floated in the center of the Sacred Circle. Spiraling down, the earth felt cool and inviting. He sensed the presence of those who died in the massacre yet could see no one. Further down, he came to a crystalline waterfall and stood under the cool water, feeling the grime of the past months wash away. Renewed, he opened his eyes and gazed into his wife's face. "Aiyani... Oh, Aiyani." She smiled at him and brushed his cheek, her touch feather soft.

Raven held the talisman in her hand as she sat next to her father, smoothing his hair and retying the bandana around his head. She looked up at Strong Eagle, who stared into the fire. "What is it?" she asked. Strong Eagle glanced away, but not before Raven saw the worry in his eyes. "Jacqo should have returned by now," she said. "Should someone go look for him?"

"Who would go?" Strong Eagle said. "We don't know the land here or even the way to Lusio's pueblo." Tossing the wood in the fire, he studied the flames. "We can't risk it."

Aponi sat on the other side of the fire, running her fingers over Etu's belt made of sweet grass. She lifted Etu to her ear, listening, then tucking the doll in her bedroll, took the bag with Chitto's prayer arrow, and slipped into the shadows.

"I'll go." Morning Dove lay curled up near the fire, eyes closed. "If he's not back by morning, I'll go." She sat up and rested her face on her knees. "This is all my fault. Dada told us to be careful when we saw cracks in the ground. But I didn't listen. Aponi tried to warn me."

Moaning in his sleep, Lusio's body twitched as he tossed and turned. The leaves packed around his wounds fell into the dirt, revealing swollen, blackened skin around the snake bites. Strong Eagle bent close to Lusio's face and examined the wounds. "Two fang marks. It was a snake with poison."

"What?" Morning Dove said.

"Lone Elk taught me once on a hunting trip. A snake that leaves two fang marks means there is poison. Four fangs are a snake without it."

"I didn't know." Morning Dove pulled leaves out of her mouth, covering the wounds on Lusio's face.

"Lone Elk said snakes can only hold a small amount of poison." He put his hand over his heart and looked to the sky. "Lusio must live."

Raven stood and looked around. "Aponi?"

"She was here…" Strong Eagle went over to Aponi's bedroll. Inside was Etu, her purple cornsilk hair tucked inside. "Her doll is here."

"Oh no," Morning Dove said. "Do you think she went to find Jacqo?"

"I'll go look for her," Strong Eagle said. "We must find her before dark." The sisters looked at each other in alarm, spittle from the leaves leaking out of the corner of their mouths.

Jacqo felt the coolness of the river as he jogged through the cottonwoods lining the shore. Dropping his musket and the skins on the ground, he lay with his face over the riverbank, scooping up water with his hands. Thirst quenched, he turned to the task of filling the waterskins. The last one full and tied to his pack, he looked up. The sun was edging west, but he had time to get back before dark. Too late, he heard a branch snap behind him.

Heart racing, Strong Eagle jogged around the large boulder, dodging cracks in the ground, sure the earth would open beneath his feet, swallowing him at any moment. He approached the sinkhole, shocked at how large it had grown, and fearing the worst, crawled on his belly and peered over the edge. "Aponi?" He was surprised to see the hole filling with water. Reaching down, fingers stretched, he could almost touch it. He inched forward, and just as his fingertips touched the water, the earth began to crumble under him. He jumped back and rolled into the same scrub where the snake had bitten Lusio. Panicked, in a flurry of flying arms and legs, he scrambled out of the brush, frantically brushing off his arms and legs.

Raven met him as he entered the camp. "Anything?"

"No. But the hole is bigger, and it's filling with water. If we can get to it, we can drink the water. But it's dangerous." He walked around the fire, looking for signs of Aponi. "There." He pointed to small footprints leading out of camp. "She went the other way."

The sky was pink and orange as Strong Eagle jogged back towards the ancient city, following Aponi's footprints. Becoming alarmed at how far she had gone, he looked up and came to an abrupt halt. In front of him, at the top of a small butte, stood Aponi. Shaking his head, he climbed to the top but stopped short, watching her.

Aponi held the stone Bear Heart had given her in her left hand and held Chitto's prayer arrow to the sky with her right as she prayed. "Bear Heart, I am afraid. Please, help us." Toes spread out on the cool limestone, she stood anchored and robust as a breeze arose, hair flying in wisps around her face. Gold flickers spiraled out of the stone, as if reaching for the sky. A moment later, she smiled and whispered: "Thank you." Tucking the stone and prayer arrow in her bag, Aponi turned, her eyes big at the sight of Strong Eagle standing there.

"What are you doing, little one?" He knelt next to her.

"Bear Heart said if I ever needed help, to call and he would come."

"He's far away, Aponi."

"It doesn't matter," she said.

THIRTY-ONE

Deep in the mountains, Bear Heart leaned against a tree, a blade of grass sticking out of his mouth as he watched wild horses graze in the corral. He wished Lusio and his family would have stayed. Bear Heart's tribe was small but strong, and they would have been a welcome addition. Yet he understood the need for family, where Lusio's daughters could know their own blood. A breeze stirred, and a shiver ran down Bear Heart's back. A dream had woken him this morning. Aponi was there, calling. Faded from his memory, he had dismissed it as he would a wandering spirit. But it nagged him. Unable to get the dream and Aponi's voice out of his head, he wandered back to seek wisdom from his wife.

Chipeta sat at the fire, watching his approach. "What worries you, husband?"

"I keep hearing Aponi's voice. Something is wrong."

"Yes, I had the same dream. Go, we'll be okay. But wait." She went into their teepee and returned carrying a bag of herbs. "Someone has been poisoned. This will help."

Gazing into her eyes, he could feel the energy stir within him as he prepared to shapeshift. Holding her chin in his hands, he studied her face, as if always to remember, and then, with the herbs tucked inside his medicine pouch, stepped into the forest, his skin rippling as black hair sprouted and his body took on the shape of a bear.

Raven and Morning Dove ran to Aponi as Strong Eagle led her back to the fire. "We were worried."

"I'm sorry." Aponi went over, retrieved Etu from her bedroll and whispered in her ear, and then snugging the doll into the bag with Chitto's spirit arrow, looked up. "It will be okay."

Aponi pulled her sleeping fur next to Lusio, lay next to him, then reached over and took his hand. As the others continued to pack the snake bites with chewed leaves, Aponi let her breath fall into sync with Lusio's and stepped into his dream.

Morning Dove pulled wet leaves out of her mouth and laid them over her father's wounds. Aponi lay on the other side, eyes closed, each breath in time with Lusio's. Wishing for the same peace she saw on their faces, she stood and joined Strong Eagle and Raven.

"We need water." Strong Eagle looked at Morning Dove. "It's too dangerous for Raven, and Aponi is with Lusio. The hole you fell into is filling with water we can use. You need to help me." He picked up the one remaining waterskin and held it up. Empty.

"I can't." Morning Dove trembled as they walked along the path.

"You're smaller. I can hold you." They came around the boulder to the sinkhole.

"What if we both fall in?" She whispered, her voice cracking.

"We must try. Lusio will die without water."

"What do I do?"

Strong Eagle tied his fishing line to the water skin and handed it to her. "Lie on your belly and crawl to the edge." Dark splotches from tears marked the ground as she scooted towards the hole.

"Good. I'll hold your feet so you won't fall."

Reaching the sinkhole, Morning Dove gasped as dirt around the edge crumbled.

"Be as still as you can." Strong Eagle said. "I've got you. "

"Please," she cried.

"Almost done. Open your eyes and look. Has the water risen enough to fill the water skin?"

"I...I... I think I can get it." Looping the line around her hand, she dropped the skin down into the water, feeling the weight as it filled. "Got it." She pulled it up and over the edge, wrapping the fishline around the top. "Oh no..." she screamed as the edge gave way, her shoulders dropping into the hole.

Strong Eagle pulled her back in a slow, steady roll from the crumbling earth, grabbing the waterskin as it bounced on the ground. He held her as she cried. "I'm sorry you had to do that. Let's go back to the fire."

"You did it." Raven hugged Morning Dove. "Thank you."

"Is this our new life?" Morning Dove asked. "Will we never have peace? Will we never feel safe?" As the darkness of night surrounded them, Raven looked up at Strong Eagle, her face a mixture of shadow and light against the fire.

He opened the last of their food cache. "Let's eat something and rest. We'll decide what to do in the morning."

Bear Heart entered the camp. Raven and Morning Dove lay huddled together, asleep, while Strong Eagle sat staring into the fire. Next to Lusio lay Aponi. "I knew you would come," she said, opening her eyes.

At the sound of Aponi's voice, Strong Eagle looked over, eyes widening at the sight of Bear Heart, now kneeling next to Lusio, and back at Aponi, who sat with a grin on her face. Lusio continued to twitch as he moaned, his body covered in a sheen of sweat.

"It's really you." Strong Eagle joined them.

"I had a dream that Aponi called for help." He took the herbs Chipeta sent out of his medicine pouch. "Poisoned?"

Strong Eagle took the saliva-soaked leaves off Lusio's wounds. "Snakebite."

Bear Heart nodded in approval. "That is good, draws out the poison." He sprinkled the herbs over each wound, then replaced the leaves. "Water?"

"We only have this." Strong Eagle held up the waterskin.

Bear Heart stared at him for a moment and then took the waterskin off his belt and poured in the rest of the herbs. He opened Lusio's mouth with his fingers and dribbled a little. "This will help." He looked over at the fire and the sleeping girls. "White boy?"

"He went to get water... hasn't returned."

Bear Heart studied Strong Eagle's face, taking in the worry. "I will find him. Keep giving these herbs to Lusio until he wakes. If he can walk, come to the river." He looked up at the moon, which was almost full. "Otherwise, I will return." His face softened looking down at Aponi. With her hand in her father's, she laid back down and closed her eyes.

Strong Eagle nodded as Bear Heart rose. "Watch out for holes that open under your feet..." But all he saw was Bear Heart's back as he jogged out of camp, followed by the rustle of bushes.

Jacqo squinted his eyes at the sun's glare coming through the trees. Unable to move his arms, he realized he was strapped to a tree. His pack with the full waterskins lay where they fell on the riverbank, and he could see the glint of his knife stuck into a tree. A tall man with long, scraggy white hair stood nearby, holding the musket to the sunlight. Jacqo feigned sleep but watched as the man went over and rummaged through his pack, pulling out the gunpowder. Wiggling his arm through the rope, Jacqo felt the ground until he touched a flat stone. Using the edge to rub, the rope began to fray and loosened.

Suddenly, branches snapped as a bear came crashing through the brush. The man raised the musket, but the bear rushed and swiped at him, leaving streaks of blood across the man's chest. A loud bang sounded as the musket fired, and amidst smoke, the tall man dropped the musket on the ground and ran, disappearing into the forest.

Jacqo felt the rope break just as the bear stumbled and fell, dripping blood on the ground as it shapeshifted back into the human form of Bear Heart. Shrugging out of the rope, Jacqo jumped up and ran to him.

"Bear Heart! What? How did you...?"

Bear Hearts' breath came in wheezes. "Aponi... she called me... said she was afraid." Bear Heart closed his eyes, his breath coming in soft gasps.

Jacqo grabbed a water skin and frantically tried to find the source of bleeding. Pouring water on Bear Heart's upper torso, he saw he had been shot in the shoulder. Ripping his shirt off, he bound Bear Heart's upper chest, putting pressure on the wound.

"Just grazed me." Bear Heart opened his eyes and looked up at Jacqo. "Get the water to Lusio."

"I can't leave you here."

"I'll be okay. Help me over to that tree you were tied up at." He sat up with Jacqo's help. "Go. When Lusio can travel, come back." He sat down with a grunt, and leaned against the tree.

Jacqo looked at Bear Heart's shoulder. The bleeding had slowed. He pulled his knife out of the nearby tree and gave it to him, along with a waterskin. "Okay. But I'm coming right back." Jacqo stood and strapped on his pack, putting the musket in the shoulder strap.

As Jacqo turned to leave, Bear Heart spoke. "I'm sorry for the trouble my daughter caused you." Jacqo stopped, listening. "I hope this makes up for it."

Jacqo turned and squatted by Bear Heart. Hands grasped, the gaze between them spoke of forgiveness that no words could express. "Hold on."

Bear Heart watched him disappear into the cottonwoods and closed his eyes. He could still feel the softness of Chipeta's face as they said goodbye.

Strong Eagle sat gazing into the fire, watching shapes of those he loved flicker in the flames, then disappear into another flame, another shape. Raven lay next to him, asleep, talisman clutched in her hand. Rubbing his fingers over the smooth, white puma tooth that hung on his chest, he reached down and touched the matching necklace that she wore around her neck, amazed they had both survived. Next to her slept Morning Dove, an occasional moan sounded as her face tightened. Across the fire lay Lusio and Aponi, their breath deep and even.

"Am I dreaming?" Lusio asked. The heady scent of lavender filled the air. In the crystalline mist of the waterfall, he saw his wife. "Aiyani?" Reaching out to touch her, he cried in despair at the empty space, desperate to feel her skin.

"Now is not the time, my husband. Our daughters need you," she whispered. The light around her brightened, and looking beyond Lusio, Aiyani smiled at her daughter's beautiful face.

"Thank you, Mama," Aponi said, gazing into the light.

In the distance, Lusio could hear Aponi's voice calling him. Confused, he looked again. As his daughter's voice grew louder, Aiyani became a faint, wavering shape, slowly disappearing into the mist.

Lusio felt a squeeze of his hand and an urgency to wake washed over him as he heard his daughter.

"Dada, wake up. I need you."

ANCIENT REUNION: BOOK THREE

SISTERS

Bear Heart drifted in and out of a dream. In one, he held Chipeta's face in his hands, saying goodbye. In another, his body shape shifted into his four-legged familiar.

Was it just yesterday?

The ground underneath him grew cold in the night, and as he woke. Wincing in pain, he reached up and felt his shoulder where the musket ball grazed him. The bleeding had stopped, but he realized his weakness as his hand dropped to the ground.

I don't want to die here... If it is my time, I want to be in Chipeta's arms...

Little by little, his skin rippled as it thickened, the stirrings of bear energy as natural to him as changing clothing. Soft dense underfur, covered with long coarse black hair, crept along his back, cushioning him against the hard bark of the tree. Picking up the knife Jacqo left for him, he cut a tuft of hair and stuck it into the tree. The fur on his body grew thicker, fingernails became claws, and he felt pressure in his face as his nose softened into a round snout. As the strength of bear filled him, he fully shape-shifted into his namesake, rose and lumbered into the trees.

Coming soon....

AUTHOR'S NOTES

The Sacred Circle

We live in a roundish world. The Earth is round. Oranges, apples, eggs, the sun, and the moon are round. Even stars seen up close are a ball of fire. We are also round: our heads, limbs, blood vessels, vital organs, breasts, and bottoms - some more than others. Trees, stones and flowers, the original wisdom of the land, are each unique in their roundness. A source of knowledge and medicine, they gather and hold knowledge sacred for thousands of years. Greek mythology gives us the labyrinth, while Celts and Scots weave their own unique relationship with elements, seasons, and animals, all connected in a circular fashion. Native Tribes of both Northern and Southern Hemispheres use The Sacred Circle, better known in modern times as The Medicine Wheel, as a foundation that holds their Spirit strong.

As a grounding philosophy, all faiths and beliefs are welcome in the circle. A sacred tool with an endless set of meanings, it helps us to organize our thoughts and actions and, in general, walk the path of Spirit. We are set upon the wheel at birth, then with the constant movement and change that is life, are taught to move around the wheel in balance, to walk gently and prayerfully on the Earth. Ancient Reunion is the story of such a journey.

The Cover

While searching public domain pictures for a photo to use on the cover, I came across the one used on this book. I immediately saw the strength and resilience, as well as compassion and gentleness I was looking for in Lusio. In the angular bones on his face and gentleness of his eyes, I knew I had found someone who knew, that to survive in this world, one must have a deep relationship with the earth. Indeed, each step is a prayer.

Special thanks to the NYPL for placing this picture in the public domain. Please read the following and follow the link if you would like to know more, or support this worthy institution.

The New York Public Library believes that this item is in the public domain under the laws of the United States. Though not required, if you want to credit us as the source, please use credit: The New York Public Library, and provide a link back to the item on our Digital Collections site. Doing so helps us track how our collection is used and helps justify freely releasing even more content in the future.

<u>Sate Sa (a Zuni governor). - NYPL Digital Collections</u>

I would like to honor the **Zuni Visitors Center Visitor and Arts Center,** as well as the **A:shiwi A:wan Museum and Heritage center,** which are both located at the Zuni Pueblo, Zuni NM. I am grateful for the time they took to talk with me, and I'm eager to return and learn more. Please explore the rich history of The Zuni and support their work.

Finally, thank you for reading. You can find me on **Facebook: Sue Paterson – Writer.** All news regarding new reading, upcoming website, etc, will be posted there. Have a lovely day.

ACKNOWLEDGEMENTS

Thea Constantine – From our early days of writing at Beaterville Café to the present, you make writing fun, inspirational and honest. Thank you for the prompt which birthed this story.

Christi Krug –From Wildfire Writing to fifteen years of mentorship, your ability to see the positive and inspire, peppered with honest critique, is priceless.

To my fellow writers in critique groups: you took me on as a novice writer, listened to my stories, and shared yours with me. Thank you to GC Troop, Connie, Jan-Marie, Chuck, Morry, Patty, Vicki and Bryan, Rick, Mark and Lori.

Viktoriya: Your eagerness to read my pages kept me writing. I still have your sticky notes from the first draft, which helped to shape the story. Thank you.

Katherine Custard and Paul LeRoq – "Just publish the damn thing..." Had it not been for your editing, support, critique, and encouragement, this story may still be filed away. Thank you.

Healers I have worked with, including Richard M, Barret Eagle Bear, Ashera S, Vilma P and many more. You will recognize some of the words on these pages. Thank you making the world a better place to be in.

Special thanks to Matt Hall for making Cover Designs look easy, Rachel Bostwick for formatting help, and Emily Paper for editing. Your patience and skills are inspiring, and makes everything look pretty.

Larry, my husband, best friend, historian and fellow journeyer. It's been an adventure, hasn't it? And to Charley and Phillip, my sons, to whom this book is dedicated. Thank you for walking this life with me and teaching me to be a better human.

Finally, to all the animals that surround me every day, convincing me that all will be better if I just step outside for a moment and walk barefoot in the grass.